The Four Caravels of Christopher Columbus

The Four Caravels
of
Christopher Columbus

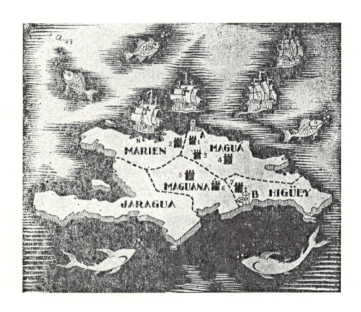

Written by Rita M. Stark

Copyright © 2005 by Rita M. Stark.

ISBN: Softcover   1-4134-7153-6

All rights reserved. No part of this book may be reproduced or transmitted in any form or by any means, electronic or mechanical, including photocopying, recording, or by any information storage and retrieval system, without permission in writing from the copyright owner.

This book was printed in the United States of America.

To order additional copies of this book, contact:
Xlibris Corporation
1-888-795-4274
www.Xlibris.com
Orders@Xlibris.com

ACKNOWLEGMENTS

Many thanks to Prof. Mark I. Little for editing assistance; to Prof. Santiago González Fernández-Corugedo, Consul of Education at the Spanish Consulate General in Miami, for special advice; to Dr. Sophie Jakowska from the University of Santo Domingo; to father Vicente Rubio Archivist at La Casa de los Altos Estudios in Santo Domingo; to Paul Fagundo and Dr. James Donalson; to Gary Herrick, "The Computer Professor"; to Helen Lamperti and Lawrence Amuso for revision.

TABLE OF CONTENTS

Preface 11
CHAPTER 1
Columbus' secret 15
CHAPTER 2
Ferdinand and Isabella 21
CHAPTER 3
The reconquest of Granada 25
CHAPTER 4
The expulsion of the Jews 29
CHAPTER 5
The documents before the departure 35
CHAPTER 6
The ships 59
CHAPTER 7
The crews 64
CHAPTER 8
Life aboard a caravel 68
CHAPTER 9
The instruments 71
CHAPTER 10
The stop at Gomera 73
CHAPTER 11
The letter to Santángel 76

CHAPTER 12
The return 85
CHAPTER 13
Annibale de Gennaro's letter 90
CHAPTER 14
Pope Alexander VI's bulls 94

TABLE OF ILLUSTRATIONS

Young Genoves 20
Ferdinand and Isabella 24
Regnü Hispanie 28
Columbus in 1492 34
Seeking Royal support 34
La Fusta 63
History of the Canary Islands 75
Columbus shows a coin to a Taíno Indian 84
Columbus received at court 88
Columbus' coats of arms 89
Demarcation lines 96

PREFACE

Columbus achieved his American discovery with not only three ships, but with four. This discovery is interesting because it reflects that history, like any other science, is not perfect, but perfective. When the data to complete a study do not give us satisfactory answers we must recur to a process of hypothesis, which is not contrary to history, but very often has no possibility of being verified. Due to the fact that this period is a key-time in world history, a study of the documents preceding the departure as well as the ones after the return becomes necessary to corroborate the presence of a fourth ship and not let the hypothesis become the principal element of our research.

In the year 1492 the most important enterprises requested by Spanish politics, to be accomplished by the Catholic Kings, were the following: the re-conquest of Granada and the expulsion of the Jews. In the discovery-conquest of the new routes to the Indies to colonize new lands it was a political, social, economical, and psychological necessity to obtain recognition from the Pope, who was in charge of allotting these "nobody's lands," to bypass the various Catholic Kings, who all deferred to the Pope.

History and Experience.

"When events follow in chronological order, they evolve in affinity with the ones that have preceded them. They depend from one another, not always and exclusively out of necessity, but like a mesh well woven rationally." These words of Emperor Marcus Aurelius Antoninus, taken from his book *"Meditations"* or *"Soliloquies,"* indicate a method to understand historic events by realizing an association between the time of our life and the historic time.

The past becomes an abstract category if we do not realize the connection with our experiences. So also past human activities can lose their meaning if we take them out of the longer historical context.

Often the experience, the direct acquaintance of the persons, and the knowledge of the motivations that have brought them to act in a certain manner require an objective understanding conditioned to the degree of intelligence, culture, and sensibility to study a certain historic period.

Very rarely two persons describe a witnessed event the same. Each records the part that has made an impression on his/her subconscious.

The XV century was a century of deep crisis in ideals. What characterizes a certain era can be discovered in a period of crisis when a choice has to be made. Old ideologies, lifestyles, and traditions are hard to kill while the newborn ideologies have not yet been able to impose themselves.

Another characteristic of crises is that they do not manifest themselves always in the same social class—an economic crisis hits always the poorest members of the population, but an intellectual crisis can manifest itself in two contradictory manners.

When an elite sets itself apart from the way the usual society is meant to be, it imposes a vision of life that is no longer real. Such an elite operates in a world completely separated from reality. This type of crisis is born each time a group of intellectuals generates ideas or actions to leave behind an imprint of power and superiority.

This phenomenon occurs each time a scientific discovery puts in jeopardy the belief of certain human and religious values considered unchangeable. The perfect example is Galileo, who challenged a millennia old belief.

It is certain, however, that no matter what the motivations or beliefs are, crises create a chain-reaction that involves the whole society. If this society is not able to react, it will be destroyed by the new forces that have emerged from the crisis and received confirmation through an entire intellectual revolution.

The element of time.

In the XV century the perception of time was completely different from the concept we have today. The Renaissance man accepted with enthusiasm everything that was attached to human experience, because it was supported by the intellect. It is the intellect that allows the individual to do "what he wants." It is in this "*Humanitas*" that the love for the Arts and the Letters reconcile with the practicality of the everyday life, intended as experience. When we realize who we are, time acquires more value and we understand the importance of our actions.

Columbus' "*sensus sui*" (= conscience of the self) had already emerged when he began thinking to his voyage of discovery, but it took the superior intelligence of a ruler to realize the most appropriate political opportunity to bring it to completion.

The man of the XV century begins to realize the advantage in actions accomplished in a rational manner even if, some time, a wait longer than expected is required. When this happens a study of the past becomes useful in our everyday lives to bring us into the future.

At this point we need to consider that Spain and Portugal were the two most apt nations on the Atlantic to sail toward a new world. From one of the two the idea to sail to the Indies was expected to be born. Every European nation was aware of this fact, because even the foreign ambassadors to the Spanish Court were proposing it. But we will explain later the reason why Spain was the nation capable of realizing this enterprise. Right now the most important factor to notice is the geographical location.

For Columbus, however, the most crucial factor was the discovery of a new *Habitat*, where new cities could be built, because his purpose was colonization, not exploitation of a natural environment so hospitable.

CHAPTER 1

COLUMBUS' SECRET

Since the age of nineteen, Columbus had navigated the waters of the Atlantic Ocean at the service of the King of Portugal. In 1481 he had started to correspond with an Italian astrologer, Paolo del Pozzo Toscanelli, who had drawn a very accurate world map indicating that the Indies could be reached not only by land, as Marco Polo had done, but also by crossing *"The Sea of Darkness."*

This astrologer sent his map with a letter to the king of Portugal's advisors and told Columbus. From the moment this information was received at court, Columbus tried numerous times to convince the king and his advisors to finance an expedition to *"buscar el Levante por el Poniente"* (= to seek the East via the West), but he was always rejected.

In 1484 something else happened that gave Columbus even more positive information about a world on the other side of the Atlantic Ocean. Alonso Sánchez de Huelva, a naval pilot also at the service of Portugal and Columbus' friend, while sailing between the Canary Islands and

Madeira, was overtaken by a terrible storm that brought the ship about seven hundred and fifty leagues away from her destination to an island in the middle of the Atlantic Ocean (thought by many to be Bermuda). From there, while returning to Portugal with only five men left in the crew, Alonso landed in Terceira,—an island in the Azores Archipelago belonging to Portugal and so called because it was the third to be discovered—where Columbus welcomed him in his home. Although some historians of the period do not accept this information because it was not exactly known whether Columbus lived in the island of Terceira, Gonzalo Fernández de Oviedo was the first author to write about this event in 1535.

"Some would have it that a caravel going to Spain from England, happened to be driven by such strong contrary winds that she was forced to sail toward the west for many days, until were discovered one or more islands near the Indies. When the sailors went ashore, they saw the natives going about naked . . . .

When the caravel started sailing toward the European coast, the winds were favorable and reached it in a very short time . . ."[1]

All the men on board had died except the captain and three or four of them, who were extremely ill and died shortly after having come ashore. It is also said that the captain was Columbus' friend and he understood astrology. He had marked the outlines of a land he had found and, in great secrecy, told Columbus about it. Columbus begged him to draw a map while he was resting

---

[1] Gonzalo Fernandez de Oviedo was a friend of Columbus and Vicente Pinzón. He went to America with the fleet of Pedraria Dávila as inspector of mines. He died in Santo Domingo in 1557. The above quotation is translated from his most important work *"Historia general y natural de las Indias, islas, y tierra firme del Mar Océano."*

in his house and being cared during his illness. He did, but died shortly after of an unknown disease like the other sailors.

In this manner Columbus found out about the new discovered land in the middle of the Atlantic Ocean and had all the coordinates to enable him to reach it. However Columbus was alone when his friend died and there was no witness to corroborate his story. De Oviedo ended his narration with these words: *"In my opinion it is a falsehood."*[2] But the historians of the era agreed upon the fact that because the captain died in Columbus' home all the papers of his ship must have been left here.

Las Casas[3] stated that from that day on Columbus had the sure knowledge that, after navigating from the Island of Hierro, in the Canary Islands, approximately seven hundred fifty leagues west, he would find land. But he kept this information a secret. The proof of this theory came during his second American voyage when on November 3, 1493, exactly seven hundred and fifty leagues west of Hierro he found a small island measuring twenty square kilometers six leagues west of Guadalupe in the French Antilles.

Some of the natives reported that Columbus had named the island *"La Desecada"* because he found it very arid and depressing. But De Oviedo and Santa Cruz gave another explanation: *"The first land he found and discovered was an island which, as soon as he saw it, he named "La Deseada" because of the desire he and his crew had to see land."*

---

[2] *Ibidem.*

[3] Bartolomé de las Casas witnessed Columbus' arrival in the Andalusian capital after his first voyage and his departure for the second. He began compiling his *"Historias de Las Indias"* in 1527 and wrote only three volumes; he finished the other three in 1561. The part of this book related to Columbus is particularly important because it is the most detailed source.

Apparently the story told by the native did not seem to be supported by any documents, while the old maps have always shown the Spanish name *"La Deseada"* and the Portuguese name of *"La Desejada"*—both words meaning the same thing. But it is true that Columbus wanted to keep the discovery of this island a secret because there is no mention of it in *The Log* and moreover, Michele da Cuneo[4], a reporter who took part in the expedition, described with great emphasis only the discovery of the other islands—Dominica, Maria Galante, and Guadalupe.

Manzano in his book *Colón descubrió America del Sur en 1494* calls Columbus *"the sole beneficiary of the great secret of the unknown pilot"* adding furthermore *"Columbus deprived his friend of the glory of a great discovery"* implying that he used the information for his own advantage.

The fact is that by the end of 1484 Columbus had in his possession very valuable documents—the letters and the map of Toscanelli and the charts of his dead friend. This was all the evidence he needed to locate land on the other side of the Atlantic Ocean.

After the death of his wife and the continuous rejection of the king of Portugal he decided to move to Castile, with his son Diego, and offer his services to the Spanish Crown.

While in Spain he learned that his exploration rivals, the brothers Pinzón, were in possession of a map drawn by Esdras, a cartographer of the period, and were also considering an expedition of discovery. However, Toscanelli's map was much more accurate and scientific. The only problem was that Columbus could not divulge to the Spanish monarchs Toscanelli's letters and map,

---

[4] Michele da Cuneo was an old friend of Columbus' family from Savona, Italy, who wrote *"Relazione di Michele da Cuneo indirizzata in ottobre 1495 al nobile concittadino Messer Gerolamo Annari."*

because they had been expressly prepared for the Portuguese court. He had to find a way to send the information secretly. He wrote to Friar Juan Pérez about his being in possession of a very important document and asked him to reveal it, secretly, to the Spanish monarchs.

Madariaga[5] writes: *"Obviously the letter friar Pérez wrote to the Catholic kings had revealed a new fact, important enough to change the course of events. Also the queen thought that it would be best to discuss in private with Friar Pérez this revelation before calling Columbus. In fact the revelation of Friar Pérez was of such nature that it settled once and for all the cosmographical aspect of Columbus' plan."*

The Spanish Monarchs received Columbus at court in January 1486 and allowed him to submit his expedition's plan of discovery. A commission of experts nominated by the crown met in Salamanca and Cordova to examine Columbus' plans. The verdict, however, was negative because the war against the Moors was still going on and depleting the treasury. The queen advised Columbus to resubmit the project to the commission at a later time.

In 1488, at his return from Portugal, Columbus had met Antonio Giraldini and they had become very good friends. Antonio, on his deathbed, recommended Columbus to his brother Alejandro encouraging him to help the Genovese. The friendship between the Admiral and Alejandro Geraldini became so great that Columbus named the discovered island of Berequeya "*Graciosa*" after his friend's mother.

Alejandro and Diego de Mendoza, who as third party mediated the dispute between Castile and Aragon in favor of Columbus, convinced the queen completely of the navigator's genius.

---

[5] Salvador de Madariaga was a Spanish diplomat, writer, and historian of liberal political tendencies who was communicating with different Embassies.

"Young Genoves"
Oil on canvas by Artist Juan Medina Ramirez
Santo Domingo

CHAPTER 2

FERDINAND AND ISABELLA

Legend has credited Queen Isabella with the financial support needed for the greatest discovery of the century, but historians have disagreed whether the credit should be given exclusively to the queen or be also shared with Ferdinand. It is sure, however, that right after the refusal of the commission of experts in 1486, Isabella met Columbus at Jaén and gave him hope that she would consider again his request as soon as circumstances would permit. She asked Columbus to remain in Spain at the expense of the Crown and supported his ideas while waiting for the war against the Moors to conclude.

From the *"Noticias Legalizadas de las Erogaciones de la Corona"* (= Legal notices of distributions from the Crown) we know that, between May 5, 1487 and August 3, 1492, the time of departure for the first voyage, Columbus was being regularly paid in maravedís. On May 5, 1487 he received 3,000 maravedís, by decree of Alonso de Quintanilla upon mandate of the Bishop of Palencia for accomplishing special tasks at the service of Their Highnesses. On August 27 of the same year Columbus received 4,000 maravedís by mandate of Their Highnesses and decree of the bishop to defray the costs of a special departure on July 3, and, on October 15, 4,000 more by mandate of Their Highnesses and decree of the bishop. On June 16, 1488 Columbus received another 4,000 maravedís by decree of Their Highnesses. In 1491 the accounting ledger of Luis de Santángel and Francisco Pinelo, Treasurers of the Fraternity, showed that Columbus had received 140,000 maravedís. This same entry appears in the accounting ledger of García Martínez and Pedro de Montemayor in the year 1492 where was also specified the reason why—"*to pay for the caravels that Their Highnesses are sending as fleet to the Indies and to pay Columbus who goes with the fleet.*"

Isabella kept her promises. She was a strong and loving woman and she admired Columbus' pride and genius. Even though she and Columbus were of the same age and of the same temperament, she never loved him. All through her life she did not know any love other than Ferdinand's. She had known times of hardship before becoming queen and she grew to be very intelligent, serious, honest, and pious. She used her intelligence to help her husband create one of the greatest kingdoms in Europe.

Her ascent to the throne of Castile had not been without lack of opposition. She owed the crown to the turbulent nobility of the kingdom who forced her brother and predecessor, Enrique IV, to resign and proclaim her sister Queen of Castile. Further more Enrique IV had to take away from his own daughter, Juana, all rights of succession.

Not less full of grave events were the circumstances that brought Ferdinand to the throne of Aragon. He was the son of Juan II and his second wife, Juana Enriquez of

Castile. Carlos de Viana, first son of Juan II and his first wife Bianca de Navarra, was the rightful heir to the throne of Aragon. Upon the death of Bianca, however, because her will did not specify the power between the surviving husband and the son heir, a long time of conflict had started. Carlos, nevertheless, had been recognized as the Lieutenant General of Navarra but the two countries had become opposite factions.

The nobility of the plains supported Juan II in wanting Ferdinand to become king, the nobility of the mountains supported Carlos. After many years of battles, Juan II acknowledged Carlos' birthright and promised him the throne and the marriage to Isabella. But Carlos died suddenly and suspicion arose about him being poisoned by his stepmother, Juana Enriquez. Now Ferdinand was left the sole heir to the throne of Aragon and was recognized as such by the *Cortes* in Catalayud in 1461 and at the death of Juan II he became King of Aragon in 1479.

At the same time in Castile, Juana, daughter of Enrique IV, who had been dispossessed of her rights of succession, had gathered many nobles, including the King of Portugal, to bring war to Isabella. This civil war ended in 1479 and it was time for Isabella to marry Ferdinand, who was substituting his dead brother in uniting the two Houses.

The nobility was against this substitution therefore the new reign began during very unfavorable times in the midst of hostilities. The new monarchs had to rule strongly and at the same time tactfully and diplomatically. The use of special concessions to gain favors from the nobility had to be abolished, due to the fact that this particular behavior had already caused the last civil war in Spain.

It was not by chance that, when Ferdinand and Isabella became Kings of Castile and Aragon, they decided to restart the war against the Moors.

Machiavelli wrote in *"The Prince"* about the Spanish monarchs and their Holy War: " . . . *it lasted a long time because of the difficulties of the situation and also because Ferdinand wanted to weaken the military strength of the nobility by keeping its soldiers occupied in the re-conquest of the Spanish territories to unite Spain and make them feel part of a military campaign led by the king himself."*

At the end of the year 1491 the re-conquest of Granada was bringing to an end the unification of Spain. But the Catholic kings were not ready to stop there. They had two other projects to accomplish in 1492: the expulsion of the Jews to bring them revenues from what they were forced to leave behind and Columbus' enterprise to solve the problems of the nobility by conveying its interests toward new rich lands to exploit.

Royal collection, London, by permission of
Her Majesty the Queen.

CHAPTER 3

THE RECONQUEST OF GRANADA

At the beginning of the VIII century Muslims invaders from North Africa began a conquest of Southern Spain and took at least three fourths of the peninsula. By the X century the caliphate of Cordoba was a very sophisticated Arab Empire that left a visible mark on the country.

A small minority of Jews managed to survive under Muslim rule by remaining neutral while Spain began a campaign of re-conquest of the lost territories.

Ferdinand III and Alfonso X regained the valley of the Guadalquivir and Murcia leaving the Muslim Spain very reduced in power as well as territory. The successor of Alfonso X, Alfonso XI, defeated definitively the Muslims in the battle of the Salado River in 1340 and took back the Fortress of Gibraltar ending this way the danger of new African invasions. The only territory left to the Muslims—of what was called Al-Andalus—was the reign of Granada, where Muhammed Ibn Nasr consolidated a dynasty that lasted until the Catholic kings began their campaign of re-conquest (1481-1492) to unify Spain.

When in 1482 the Spanish *Cortes* gave their consent to a definitive final campaign against the Kingdom of the Moors, pope Sixtus IV acknowledged with a papal bull this enterprise as a crusade and sent an appeal to the Christians of France, England, Germany, Switzerland, and even Poland to unite with the Spaniards *"who were committed to re-conquer Granada and every meter of Spanish territory still under the domination of the infidel."*

The Moorish king in vain asked for help from the Sultan of Constantinople, Bayazid II, who limited himself to complain to the pontiff about the cruelties and the violent pillages the Spaniards were inflicting on the Muslims in the cities they had conquered and threatened to retaliate on the Christians living in his Sultanate.

Ferdinand and Isabella answered the pope that the territories occupied by the Moors were property of their ancestors and the King of Granada had no legal jurisdiction over them. The Sovereigns were simply defending the Christians living in these territories: therefore this war was becoming a legitimate defense of Christianity. The retaliations of Sultan Bayazid II in the Orient were no concern of Spain.

In 1483 another Moorish king was reigning: Boabdil I. He had been captured by the Spaniards but released under the following conditions:

1. He had to declare himself a subject of the Kingdom of Castile.
2. He had to pay a tribute of 12,000 gold doubloons.
3. He had to free 400 Christian prisoners.
4. He had to allow free transit to the Christian army through his territory.
5. He had to promise to appear at court each time he was summoned.

6. He had to send his son as hostage to some members of the Spanish nobility.
7. He had to respect a truce of two years.

But king Boabdil did not respect the last condition of the treaty and declared "Holy War" on Spain. Boabdil was defeated and the city of Granada capitulated on November 25, 1491 and was handed over to the Spanish monarchs within sixty-five days from the capitulation.

On January 2, 1492, two hours before daylight, the two most important dignitaries of the province came to the city with horses and infantry. A Moor named Monier and another named Alben Maiar showed the Spanish dignitaries some secret passages to the Alhambra through back streets. Then Monier opened the main gates and let the Spanish soldiers in. Boabdil left the fortress with a garrison of 600 soldiers. He rode to the mountainside of his beloved city to take the last view of it and bid farewell with a great sigh. The location where he turned his horse around to leave Spain forever became known as *"El último suspiro del Moro."* (= The Moor's last sigh).

The Christian army, after taking possession of the palace, erected an altar and celebrated Mass. They also raised a huge cross on the highest tower of the city and everybody acclaimed.

Among the acclaiming crowd was also Christopher Columbus, who now felt that it was the right time to reinforce his request of support for the discovery of the new lands to import spices and gold to refurbish the Royal Treasury.

This conquest completely satisfied the emotions and the fantasy of the XV century man, who had lived for many years preoccupied with the presence of the infidel in his land.

With the conquest of Granada and the unification of Spain, Isabella and Ferdinand had acquired great prestige in the eyes of the world and had been recognized as "The Catholic Kings." They wanted to maintain this image and were beginning to plan a crusade to help the Italians with their problems with the Turks, who still possessed Otranto on the Adriatic Sea. Columbus was very aware of that; therefore he began to emphasize religion and colonization to make them play an important role in this voyage of discovery. He wrote the Spanish king a letter stating: *"I declare to Their Highnesses that all the income generated by my enterprise can be spent to conquer the infidel."*

CHAPTER 4

THE EXPULSION OF THE JEWS

Toward the end of the XV century the word *"Infidel"* was not describing only the Moors or the Muslims but also anyone of another religion who opposed Christianity. These persons did not have any civil rights. Special privileges—besides the ones offered by the common laws—could be given to them by private civic communities but revocable at any time without a plausible explanation.

Just to give an example, a Spanish Jew was simply a Jew born in Spain by chance. He had nothing in common with his compatriots. Relations between Jews and Christians were limited by the Christian canon laws and kept to a minimum or forbidden altogether. The many voices raised in favor of religious tolerance were never heard.

Only the *"Infidel"* who had been converted to Christianity could enjoy all the civil rights of a Christian community. The Jews were tolerated: the sporadic periods of persecution were based on events like epidemics, famine, earthquakes, and floods believed to be a divine punishment for a society admitting the presence of non-believers.

These specific situations offered people the opportunity to rob the ghettos, kill, and loot the members of the Jewish community. Such riots happened against the will of the authorities and, particularly in Spain, against the will of the monarchs, who had adopted pro-Semitic political policies.

But during the second half of the XV century a new slow change in politics occurred with the birth of the National States. They characteristically centralized power in the hands of rulers thereby making all laws equal for everyone in the territory. They also took away from the nobility all privileges and invited them to court to control them better and reduce cause for rebellion.

As the monarchy became more and more consolidated, it enforced religious observances and the cults were suppressed. It became apparent that a plausible pretext to eliminate these contrary forces within the nation needed to be found.

Religious unity brought spiritual consolidation in Spain. Also the possibility of taking all the Jewish community's riches accumulated during centuries and the non-restitution of loans, made to the crown during the war against the Moors, became the main reasons for the monarchs to become malevolent toward the Jews. In fact the Jewish community could enjoy religious freedom—due to their enormous economic prosperity—while the members of the lower Spanish classes, who had not been able to accumulate wealth, envied them.

The Jews were also practicing usury, which was prohibited by Christian laws because the earnings from lending money were calculated by the time of the loan and time was considered to be a gift of God and not a human possession. Usury involved a speculation on something that did not belong to man. Nevertheless usury remained a monopoly of the Jews for a century and the term "*Jew*" became synonymous with a person who lent money at a high rate of interest, not just a believer of another faith.

Another monopoly of Spanish Jews was the administration of the crown's fiscal department. This made them even more hated by the Spanish people, because the Jews were charged with collecting taxes, even to the point of using force.

The Christian population, being superior in number and convinced of their religion's transcendence, knew that the Jews, even if converted, would never be completely assimilated. So the "*Edict of Expulsion*" was presented-by as an act of thankfulness to God for making Spain victorious over another crusade against the "*Infidel.*"

Even though the regions of Castile and Aragon kept their own autonomous laws after Isabella's marriage to Ferdinand, the Tribunal of the Inquisition was a powerful weapon over all of Spain. This religious instrument had already unified Spain even before the real union took place and its goal was to attack the Jews who would not convert. So Jews had to practice in secret their religion and, on the other hand, give the impression of complying with the religious practices requested by a Christian society.

The processes of the Inquisition, which had originally started only against the Jews, began to include everyone who was not Catholic. Whoever did not want to convert was considered an offender of the clergy and therefore accused of heresy. It is believed that the idea of a mass expulsion of the Jews had originated during the time when Tomás de Torquemada was Great Inquisitor.

The monarchs, however, considered the re-conquest of Granada from the Moors more important and they borrowed from Jews huge sums of money for this endeavor. At the same time the Jewish community felt that by helping Spain in this religious war they would be better accepted in the Spanish society. But it was not so.

The most rich Israelite, Don Isaac Abrabanel, had been charged with pleading this cause, by inducing the most cultured church doctors and rabbis to formulate an exposé of Jewish history in Spain during the past centuries. But in doing this they were not realizing that, even if born in Spain, they were still considering themselves guests and foreigners in a nation that in reality was their homeland. In fact their strict belief in maintaining the traditions of their ancestors kept them at Spanish society's margins.

So on March 31, 1492 the *"Edict of Expulsion"* was officially announced all over Spain. Even though its context was based on the idea of uniting Spain through religion, this mass expulsion brought immense financial gains and even more prestige for the monarchs of *"defensores fidei."* (= Defenders of the Faith).

However this new title for the Catholic kings would not be acknowledged in other European nations. When the bull of Pope Alexander VI assigned to Ferdinand and Isabella jurisdiction over the lands in the New World, this decision was not based on the expulsion of the Jews but solely on the re-conquest of Granada. The evicted, in fact, sought protection from the Vatican and the Pope placed them in the Italian territories belonging to the Church known as the Pontifical States. The edict was also valid in Sardinia, Sicily, and the Kingdom of Naples, which were possession of Spain ruled by Ferdinand's brother, Don Ferrante, King of the Two Sicilies.

It is not certain how much monetary gain this expulsion brought to the Spanish Crown, but according to information based on data provided by Abrabanel and Abraham Senior—Comptrollers General of Taxation—more than three hundred thousand families had to sell their possessions at extremely low prices because they were not allowed to take with them anything more that the bare necessities. The deadline for this evacuation was set for July 31, 1492, but it was changed to August 2, 1492 for political reasons.

Already the repercussions of the Inquisition as well as the disappearance of the Arab culture in Spain generated an internal social division. The Arabs were masters in Science and Medicine, disciplines very much in demand all over the world but only available in Spain: therefore Spain lost all the possible contacts that were depending on them. Once the Jews had left, on one side there was the rich nobility and on the other the increasing poverty of the people because of the lack of that kind of bourgeoisie with spirit of initiative and commercialism that was able to meet the requirements of both classes. The mercantile future of Spain was based on the Jews who had created a commercial bourgeoisie capable of supporting the nation's economy. The nobility, used to luxury and idleness interrupted only by military campaigns, was not able to play such a role.

Columbus' enterprise was fulfilling the dreams of the poor as well as the nobility in discovering a new world that could be exploited. But at this time, not knowing what the new lands could offer in terms of colonization, everyone's goal was strictly to import slaves, spices, and gold with the hope that this great enterprise could bring a better plan of colonization in the future.

Columbus in 1492
Courtesy of the Columbus Philatelic Society

Courtesy of the Columbus Philatelic Society

CHAPTER 5

THE DOCUMENTS BEFORE THE DEPARTURE

After the Spanish victory over the Moors, Isabella sent Columbus an extra 20,000 maravedís "*to buy decent clothes to go on a visit to Their Highnesses*" (excerpt from Las Casas) and invited him to the court. The queen's special invitation and the extra money made Columbus realize that the Sovereigns were ready to take action.

Upon suggestion of Marchena and Antonio Giraldini, who were the papal ambassadors in Spain during the time of the war against the Moors, the queen submitted Columbus' plans to a commission of Grandees, instead of scientists and theologians. The idea finally was accepted for three positive reasons. First the expedition's cost was not very high. Secondly the risk of compromising lives was also low, so in case of death the Sovereigns would not be criticized too severely. Thirdly, in case of success, the advantages would be enormous for the economy and the international politics of the nation. The discovery of new routes to the Indies was going to enhance even more the Spanish Crown's prestige across Europe and, internally, to unite under the crown those citizens, who were still unassimilated.

Furthermore the city of Palos had been sentenced to equip the monarchs' two caravels with arms and supplies for a year's term, because its citizens had committed crimes against them. The remainder of the money and goods had to be provided by the Councilors and local bankers. Furthermore, the monarchs were also considering using the same forces the nobility had provided for the reconquest of Granada so they would not remain idle.

In such a light the discovery of America seemed to be a very well-calculated risk instead of a dream.

Also, Columbus had many *"protectors"*—as he used to call his supporters—at court. The most important supporter was Luis de Santángel who was *"Escribano de ración"* (position similar to a Minister of Finances), Friar Juan Pérez, Friar Diego Deza, the Duke of Medinaceli, Alonso de Quintanilla, Francesco Pinelli, and other Italian bankers to whom the Sovereigns had been indebted for a long time. But at this time the financial situation of the crown had largely improved because of the massive expropriation of the Jews' assets and the advantages received from the conquest of Granada. By June 1492 it had been agreed on financing Columbus' expedition for the sum of 2,000,000 maravedís as long as the navigator's interest would coincide with the crown's.

Two very important documents indicate the official beginning of Columbus' expedition—*Las Capitulaciones de Santa Fe de la Vega de Granada, (April 17, 1492) y La Cédula real (April 30, 1492)* and five *Provisiones* (= ordinances).

Las Capitulaciónes de Santa Fe are called this way because, while Ferdinand was in Granada fighting the Moorish king, he ordered the construction of a small city within the walls of Granada that was called Santa Fe after a fire had destroyed the Christian camp. Before the conquest of Granada, Columbus had met here with the king and many other important personalities, who were forming a commission presided by Fr. Hernando de Talavera, with Rodrigo Maldonado, Rodrigo de Alcocer, Mendoza and Giraldini. Juan Manzano,[6] a specialist in the study of the Admiral's personality, writes *"Probably Mendoza and Giraldini were the most ardent defenders of the Admiral's cause in Santa Fe."* The proposal was voted down because the commission thought that Columbus did not have enough experience.

The theologians, who had studied Columbus' plan, had judged him a heretic because Bishop Nicolás de Lira believed that the orient ended at the Fortuna islands and St. Augustine believed that the Antipodes did not exist. So Columbus decided to submit his plan to the King of France.

Isabella, who was defending his cause but could not go against the majority of the vote, was exalted by Columbus with these words to Prince Juan: *"Everyone is a disbeliever, while our Lord has given to the Queen, our Lady, spirit, intelligence, and great power, and I am telling you that she is for me a dear and much beloved daughter. The ignorance of all the others transforms knowledge into an inconvenient fable."*

This citation and the fact that Columbus wanted to present his project to the court of France was very favorable to Isabella during the third meeting in Santa Fe[7], which made the commission finally decide upon the fact that Columbus should still remain in Spain. To the Archbishop of Seville, Diego de Deza, the Archbishop of Granada, Fr. Hernando de Talavera, and Cabrero, is due the triumph

---

[6] FCO. José Arnaiz, S.J.; *Más Luces que Sombras, Chapter 7, p. 55. Editora Amigo del Hogar, August 1989. Santo Domingo, Republica Dominicana*

[7] Alejandro Geraldini: *Cristóbal Colón: Siete Años Decisivos de su Vida. (1485-1492). pp. 315-322, Editora Arzobispado de Santo Domingo, 1987.*

of the Admiral. But Luis de Santángel was the one who urged the queen to support Columbus' brilliant scientific arguments and Columbus returned to Santa Fe after he received letters from the queen. Juan de Coloma was the registrar of all the documents. Manzano writes: "*Louis de Santángel convinced the queen; Fray Diego de Deza and Cabrero convinced the king.*" With this act began the "Spanish-Columbian Period" in the History of Spain.

Instrument of capitulation between their Catholic Majesties and Christopher Columbus
Santa Fe de la Vega de Grenada, 17 April 1492.
(AGI Patronato 295, ramo 2) fol.

"This is a transcript faithfully taken from an instrument of capitulation of the King and Queen, our lords, signed by their royal names and sealed with their seal of red wax and examined and signed by certain names of their officers, addressed to the magnificent Lord Christopher Columbus, Almirante. (The word Almirante derives from the Arab "Amir-al-ma" which means "Emir of the sea" having jurisdiction over the armadas and all kinds of vessels and galleys). *The contents of this instrument, verbatim, are as follows: this transcript was requested of me, Rodrigo Peres, scribe and notary public in the city Ysabela, by the King and Queen, our lords, for the said lord Admiral reading thus: forasmuch as his lordship the Admiral had to send the said instrument of capitulation to the Kingdoms of Castile, through which he had to pass, and go by sea many days and longtime, because of the long road from this said city to the said Kingdoms of Castile, and because at sea there are very great perils, and it could happen that the ship or ships in which the said writings were, could be lost, God forbid. So it was asked, and I, the scribe, was asked to make a transcript of the said instrument of capitulation, so that it might remain here in this city or where his lordship might please to have it in case the said original instrument were lost in any way that might or could occur. The said transcript*

or transcripts, which thus remain or might remain, could and would attest before their Royal Highnesses or before any other persons, both justices or others of any law or estate or condition, that I, the scribe, seeing what his lordship asked me, made the transcript of the said instrument of capitulation, each chapter, one after the other, according as Their Majesties had given and authorized, the contents of which are as follows and say thus:

1) The things published and which Your Highnesses give and authorize to Christopher Columbus in partial satisfaction for what he will discover in the Ocean Seas and of the voyage which now, God helping, he is to make over them in service to Your Highnesses are those as follows:

First Your Highnesses in your capacity as lords of the said Ocean Seas make as now to the said Christopher Columbus their Admiral, in all those islands and main lands, which by his hand and industry are discovered or he may win in the said Ocean Seas, for his lifetime and after he is dead to his heirs and successors from one to another in perpetuity, with all those preeminences and prerogatives pertaining to the office and according to which Alonso Enriquez, our High Admiral of Castile, and others of his predecessors in the said office, held in their districts.—*May it please their Highnesses: Juan de Coloma.*

Also Your Highnesses make the said Christopher Columbus your Viceroy and Governor—General in the entire said main lands and islands that he may discover and win in the said seas. And as for the government of each and any of them, he would make a selection of three persons for each office. Your Highnesses will select one, who can serve you best and so the lands, which our Lord will permit him to find and win for Your Highnesses, can be better ruled: *Juan de Coloma.*

Item, all and any merchandise, even if it be pearls, precious stones, gold, silver, spices, and any other things and merchandise of any kind, name and manner at all, that are bought, traded, found, earned, and exist within the limits of the said Admiralty, which henceforth Your Highnesses mercifully do grant to the said Christopher

Columbus, and wish for him to have and keep for himself the tenth part of everything, deducting all the costs that were incurred, so that what remains free and clear, he may have and take the tenth part for himself and do with it what he wishes, leaving the other nine parts for Your Highnesses. May it please Your Highnesses: Juan de Coloma. (f.v)

Also if because of the merchandise he may bring from the said islands and main lands which, as it has been stated, may be won or discovered, or from those things exchanged here for those things taken there, there should arise any litigation with other merchants, in the place where the said commerce or deal takes place and exists, indeed by the preeminence of his office of Admiral it will be proper to learn of such litigation. May it please Your Highnesses that he or his lieutenant and no other judge may know of such litigation and so it is provided henceforth. May it please Your Highnesses that it belongs to the said office of Admiral, in accordance with what was held by the said Admiral Alonso Enriquez and his other antecedents in their districts, to be just. Juan de Coloma.

Item, in all ships fitted for the said trade and negotiation, each and when, however many times they are fitted, the said Christopher Columbus may, if he wishes, contribute and pay the eighth part of all that may be spent in the outfitting and that he may also have and bear of the profit the eighth part of what results from such fleet. May it please Your Highnesses. Juan de Coloma.

These authorized and dispatched with the replies of your Highnesses at the end of each chapter in the city of Santa Fe de la Vega de Grenada this seventeenth of April of the year of the birth of our Savior Jesus Christ of Fourteen Hundred Ninety-Two.

I THE KING—I THE QUEEN

By order of the King and the Queen: Juan de Coloma. Registry of Calcena.

This transcript of the original instrument of capitulation was made in the noble city of Ysabela *on the Island of Española on the sixteenth day of the month of December, year of birth of our savior Jesus Christ Fourteen Hundred Ninety-Five, to which were called as witnesses secretaries who besought to correct and consult this said instrument of capitulation with the said original and it goes certain and true: Rafael Castaño, neighbor of the city of Seville, and Adan de Marquina, neighbor of the city of Guernicayz, and Pedro Salcedo, neighbor of the city of Fuensaldaña, and Francisco de Madrid, neighbor of the city of Madrid, who were present for all this.*

I, Rodrigo Perez, notary public in the said city Ysabela, by the grace of the King and Queen, our Lords, had this letter of transcript made and written and I was present in union with the said witnesses on seeing and arranging and correcting with the original. I testify.

And finally I sign here as token of truth: Rodrigo Peres, Notary public."

NOTE: This document is published in Navarrete I, document V, pp. 302-303. There is another version in the Archivo General de Indias in the register books of legal papers, *Indiferente General 413, Book 1, folio 192 F and V.*

We have chosen the most accurate, which is stored in the archives of "La Casa de los Altos Estudios" in Santo Domingo, Dominican Republic.

Royal License appointing Christopher Columbus Captain of the three caravels that are going to discover through the Ocean Sea.

Grenada, 30 April 1492 (A.G.S. General Stamp Registry. Year 1492.

"The Lord Ferdinand and the Lady Isabella etc. to all and whomever, captains, masters, patrons, boatswains, and sailors of naos, caravels, and fustas and to any other persons of any condition whatever, who may-be our subjects vassals, or natives to whom the below herein contained may pertain and to each and every of you to whom this our letter may be shown, or a transcript of it signed by a notary public, health and greetings.

Know that we have sent Christopher Columbus to go with certain fustas of the fleet to certain parts of the Ocean Sea on matters very complaisant to the service of God and ourselves and for this purpose we have commanded to give him and given him charge to take three ships that are needful to our subjects and natives to go on this voyage. Therefore, for the present we order all and each one of you, the said masters and patrons and sailors and companies of the said caravels and fustas, to have and hold for our captain of the said ships and fustas the said Christopher Columbus, and to obey him and hold him as our captain and do and comply and place in action everything that he may say and command to you on our behalf. All that in everything and in each part, in true form and manner, and at the time and moment, and under the penalties that he may command and impose on our behalf, not using any excuses or slowing things down, but doing everything as if we ourselves ordered it. And we, at the present, make him our captain of such ships and fustas, and *we give him power and facilities to command and govern them as our captain, and to execute in their company whatever penalties they may befall and incur for not complying and obeying his commands as aforesaid, but it is our mercy and will for the said Christopher Columbus and for you and for any one of you must not go to La Mina, or deal with it, that the most serene King of Portugal our brother holds, because our will is to keep and have kept by our subjects and natives what we have agreed and assented with the said King of Portugal our brother, about the said La Mina. We order you to do and comply under pain of our mercy and the confiscation of your goods for our chamber and exchequer: given in our city of Grenada 30 April 1492."*

I THE KING—I THE QUEEN.

I Juan de Coloma secretary of the King and Queen our Lords, had it written by their order.
(In the lower margin to the left):"So that Christopher Columbus may be obeyed as captain of your Highnesses."[8]

Provision of their catholic majesties to Christopher Columbus granting him the titles of Admiral, Viceroy and Governor of the Islands and Main Lands that he might discover.
Grenada 30 April 1942

---

[8] Text taken from Juan Pérez de Tudela: *Revista de Indias, Instituto Gonzalo Fernandéz de Oviedo.* Consejo Superior de Investigaciones Cientificas. Year 13, No 54, October-December 1953, pp 609-610. *La Mina was a fortress belonging to Portugal on the coast of Guinea.*

The Lord Ferdinand and the Lady Isabella by the grace of God, King and Queen of Castile, Leon, Aragon, Sicily, Grenada, Toledo, Valencia, Galicia, Majorca, Seville Sardinia, Cordova, Corsica, Murcia, Jaén, of the Algarves, Algesirs, Gibraltar, and the Canary Islands; Count and Countess of Barcelona; Lord and Lady of Biscay and Molina, Duke and Duchess of Athens and Neopatria; Count and Countess of Rousillon and Cerdaña, Marquis and Marchioness of Oristán and of Gociano: forasmuch as you, Christopher Columbus, go by our command to discover and win with some of our fustas, and with our people, certain islands and mainland in the Ocean Sea, and it is hoped that, God helping, some of these islands will be discovered and won, along with mainland, by our hand and industry. It is a just and reasonable thing that since you expose yourself to the said peril in our service, you should be remunerated for it. Wanting to honor you and do you mercy for the above said, it is our grace and will, that you, said Christopher Columbus, after you have discovered and won the said islands and mainland in the said Ocean Sea or any other, that you be our Admiral of the said islands and mainland which you may discover and win. You be our Admiral and Viceroy and Governor in them, and so you may henceforth call and entitle Sir Christopher Columbus and thus your sons and successors in the said office and charge they may be entitled and called Sir, and Admiral, and Viceroy, and Governor thereof so that you may use and exercise the said office of Admiralty with the said office of Viceroy and Governor of the said islands and land which thus you may discover and win for you and for your lieutenants, and hear and deliberate all litigation and civil or criminal cases touching on the said office of Admiralty and Viceroy and Governor according as the Admirals of our kingdoms are accustomed to use and exercise. You may punish and chastise the delinquents, and you may use the said offices of Admiralty and Viceroy and Governor, you and your said lieutenants in all concerns annexed to the said offices and each of them. You may have and carry-on the rights and salaries of the said offices and to each one of them annexed and pertinent as our Chief Admiral in the Admiralty of our Kingdoms of Castile, the Viceroys, and Governors of our said kingdoms bear them and are accustomed to bear them. And by this our letter or by its transcript, signed by a notary public, we command prince John, our very dear and very beloved son, and the princes, dukes, prelates, marquises, counts, masters of the orders, priors, prefects, and those of our Council and judges of our Audencia, mayors and other justices whomever of our houses and court and chancery and the sub-prefects, castles' wards, strong houses, and plain ones, and all the counselors, assistants, royal correctors, mayors, constables, sheep-judges, aldermen, knights, jurors, squires, officers and good men of all the cities and towns, villages, and places of our kingdoms and lordships and those which you may conquer and win. To the captains, masters, boatswains, officers, sailors, seamen, our subjects and natives, who are now or henceforward will be, and to each one and any of them, that the said islands and land being discovered and won by you in the said ocean sea, and made by you or by whom your power may have the oath and solemnity which in such case is required, that you have and hold from henceforward and for all your life, and after you your son and successor and from successor to successor in perpetuity, for our Admiral of the said Ocean Sea, and for Viceroy and Governor in the said islands and mainland which you the said Christopher Columbus may discover and win, and may use for yourself and for your said lieutenants that, by our said offices of Admiralty and Viceroy and Governor may place, in all which concerns them and you, they pay and have paid with quittance and rights and other things annexed and pertaining to said offices. That they keep and will keep for you all the honors, graces and mercies and liberties, preeminences, prerogatives, exemptions, immunities and all the other things and each one of them, which by reason of the said offices of Admiral, Viceroy, and Governor you should have and enjoy and which should be kept for you, all well and compliantly so that you will not therefore lack of anything. That in it or in any part of it no obstacle or opposition be set against you, or consent to set against you. Now we, by this our letterform henceforth we make you the grace of the said offices of Admiralty, Viceroy and Governor by oath of inheritance forever, and we give you the possession and near-possession of them and each one of them and power and authority to use and exercise and bear the rights and salaries thereof and of each annexed and pertaining, in accordance with what has been said. Concerning all that it has been said, if necessary for you and if you should request it, we order to our chancellor and notaries, and to the other officers who are on the boards of our seals, that they give and release to you and pass and seal our letter of rolling privilege, the strongest, stoutest, firmest, and sufficient that you ask for and that you may need. And the ones *or the others do not nor will not do wrong therefore for any manner, under pain of our mercy and of ten thousand maravedis for our chamber to everyone who may do the contrary. As for the rest we order anyone to whom this our letter is shown, and challenge them so that they appear before us in our court, wherever we may be, from the day they are challenged by the next fortnight immediately following, under the said penalty, under which we order any notary public, who may be called for this, that he shall give right therefore to the one who may present testimony, signed with his signature, so that we may know how our orders are being complied with. Given in our city of Grenada of the 30th of April in the year of the birth of the savior Jesus Christ Fourteen ninety-two.*

I THE KING—I THE QUEEN

I Juan de Coloma, Secretary of the King and of the Queen, our Lords, had it written by their order. Agrees in form. Redericus, Doctor. Registered (Examined): Sebastian de Olano. Francisco de Madrid, Chancellor.

Provision for the neighbors of Palos to give the two caravels ordered to them by the royal council[9]

Grenada 30 April 1492 (A.G.I. Patronato 295, No. 3) Fol.r/ The Lord Ferdinand and the Lady Isabella, by the grace of God, King and Queen of

---

[9] Published in Navarrete I, document No. 7 pp. 305-307 Co. Do. In/Am. Oc. I. 28, pp. 101-104. Prior text taken from Navarrete I, doc. #6 pp. 304-305.

Castile, Leon, Aragon, Sicily, Grenada, Toledo, Valencia, Galicia, Majorca, Sardinia, Cordova, Corsica, Murcia, Jaén, the Algarves, Algecirs, Gibraltar, the Canary Islands: Count and Countess of Barcelona, Lord and Lady of Biscay and Molina; Duke and Duchess of Athens and Neopatria; Count and Countess of Roussillon and Gociano.

To you, Diego Rodriguez Prieto and all other persons who are your companions and other neighbors of the city of Palos and each one of you, health and grace.

You know well how by some things done and committed by you to our disservice, you were condemned by our council to serve us for two months with two fitted caravels at your own cost and expenses each, and when and wherever we may command, under certain penalties, in accordance with all that is contained in greater detail in the said sentence which was given against you. And now, inasmuch as we have ordered Christopher Columbus to go with three fleet caravels to certain parts of the Ocean Sea as our Captain on certain matters to be fulfilled in our service, and we want him to take with him the two caravels with which you are to serve us. Therefore we order you that from the day which by this letter of ours you may be required, up to the first ten days following, without our requiring any more, nor consulting, nor awaiting, nor having another letter of ours on the subject, you will have prepared and placed in readiness the said two caravels, as you are obligated to by dint of the said sentence, to leave with the said Christopher Columbus where we order him to go. You will depart with him from the said period forth, according and when you may be told and ordered by him on our behalf, for we order him to pay you then a salary for four months for the people to go on the said caravels at the price that may be paid to the other people who may go on the said three caravels and on the other caravel that we have ordered him to take, which is the one that is commonly accustomed to be paid on that coast to the people who go as a navy on the sea. And having departed thus, you will follow the route by which he may send you on our behalf, and you will comply with his orders and go under his command and governance, provided that neither you nor the said Christopher Columbus nor any others of those who are on the said caravels go to La Mina [Portuguese port and fortress on the coast of Guinea] *nor to deal with it, as it is held by the most serene King of Portugal, our brother, because our wish is to keep and have kept what we have agreed to and capitulated with the said king of Portugal on the subject. And bringing you signed testimony of the said captain on how happy he has been with your service on the said two fitted caravels, we will hold you relieved of the said penalty, which was imposed on you by our council. Henceforth until then and thenceforth until now, we give and hold ourselves as well served by you on the said caravels for the time and according as by those of our said council it was ordered for you with the notice that we serve you that if you do not do thus or if you put up some excuse or delay, we will order to execute on you and each one of you and on your goods, the penalties contained in the said sentence which was given against you. The ones and the others must not do anything otherwise*

in any manner under pain of our mercy and of each ten thousand maravedís for our chamber, under which fine we order any notary public who may be called for this, to give to any other that you present, testimony signed with his signature so that we may know how our command is being carried out.
Given in our city of Grenada the 30th day of the month of April year of the birth of our Savior Jesus Christ, Fourteen Ninety-Two.

I THE KING—I THE QUEEN

I Juan de Coloma, secretary of the King and Queen our Lord and Lady, had this written upon their command. (Original).

Royal provisions to make available to Christopher Columbus, who was taking three caravels to certain parts of the Ocean, whatever he might need for repairing and provisioning them.[10]

Grenada, 30 April 1492 (A.G.I. Patronato 295, No 4) Fol. r/ The Lord Ferdinand and the Lady Isabella, by the grace of God, King and Queen of Castile, Leon, Aragon, Sicily, Grenada, Toledo, Valencia, Galicia, Majorca, Seville, Sardinia, Cordova, Corsica, Murcia, Jaén, the Algarves, Algesirs, Gibraltar, the Canary Islands, Count and Countess of Barcelona, Lord and Lady of Biscay and Molina, Duke and Duchess of Athens and Neopatria; count and countess of Rousillion and Cerdeña: marquis and marchioness of Oristan and Goceano.

To you, the councils, judges, assistants, mayors, constables, sheep judges, aldermen, knights, jurors, squires, officers and good men as well of cities and towns and places on the seacoast of Andalusia, as of all our kingdoms and seignories, and any other whatsoever gentlemen and persons of whatever state or condition who are our vassals, subjects and natives and to each and any of you to whom this our letter may be shown or a transcript thereof signed by a notary public, health and grace. Know that we have ordered Christopher Columbus to go with three fitted caravels to certain parts of the Ocean Sea as our captain concerning some matters to fulfill our service. Therefore we order you, each and everyone, in our place and jurisdictions, that all that the

---

[10] Published in Navarrete I, documento No. VIII, p. 307.

said Christopher Columbus wants or needs, lumber or carpenters or rigging and provision of bread and wine and fish and gunpowder or ammunitions or other things to fit, prepare, renovate, rig, repair, or supply the said caravels with which he sails be given to him. And a few other things give them to him from wherever they are found, our said captain paying for all that he may take and have need of, at reasonable prices and therein and in any matter therein do not hinder or consent to placing any obstacle or delay because he thus fulfills our service. And the ones and the others are therefore not to do this in any way, under pain of our mercy and ten thousand maravedís each for our exchequer.
Given in our city of Grenada 30 April, year of the birth of our Lord Jesus Christ Fourteen Ninety-Two.

I THE KING—I THE QUEEN

I Juan de Coloma, secretary of the King and the Queen our Lord and Lady, had this written upon their order. (On the back it is sealed with the royal seal and says as follows:
"Agreed: Rodericus, Doctor. Examined: Sebastian de Olano, Francisco de Madrid, Chancellor. Payment: Nil." (Original).

Provision of the Catholic Kings ordering suspension of recognition of crimes and cases against those who are going with Christopher Columbus until their return.[11]

---

[11] Published in: Navarrete I, documento No IX pp 307-308 Co. Do. In. Am. Oc. I 38 pp 107-109.

Grenada 30 April 1492 (A.G.I. Patronato 295 No. 5) Fol.r/ The Lord Ferdinand and the Lady Isabella, by the grace of God, King and Queen of Castile, Leon, Aragon, Grenada, Toledo, Valencia, Galicia, the Majorcas, Seville, Sardinia, Cordova, Corsica, Murcia, Jaén, the Algarves, Algecirs, Gibraltar and the Canary Islands; count and countess of Barcelona, Lord and Lady of Biscay and Molina, Duke and Duchess of Athens and Neopatria, Count and Countess of Roussillion and Cerdaña; Marquis and Marchioness of Oristán and Gociano.

To those of our council and judges of our court, judges, assistants, mayors and constables, sheep-judges and any other justices of whatever cities and towns, and villages and places of our kingdoms and seignories and each and everyone of you to whom this our letter may be shown, or its transcript, signed by a notary public, health and grace. Know that we order Christopher Columbus to go to the part of the Ocean Sea, some things in compliance with our service: and to carry the people he needs in three caravels that he is taking, he says it is necessary to give assurance to the person who are to go with him because otherwise they would not want to go with him on the said voyage. On his part it was requested from us that we should order it to them or as our mercy might be and we decided it was good. And by the present we give assurance to all and whatever persons who may go on the said caravels with the said Christopher Columbus, on the said voyage he is making by our order to the part of the said Ocean Sea, as is said, so that there will not be done to them any ill or harm or injury whatever to their persons or goods or anything that is theirs by reason of any crime they may have committed up to the day of the date of this our letter and during the time that they may be there, to their return to their houses and for two months afterward, because we order you all and every one of you, in your places and jurisdictions, not to recognize any criminal case touching the persons who may go with the said Christopher Columbus in the said three caravels during the time above said, because our mercy and will is that all this be thus suspended; and the ones and the others not make or do anything else in any way, under pain of our mercy and of ten thousand maravedís for our exchequer on each one who may do otherwise. We further order any notary public who may be called for this to give then to anyone who shows it to you, signed testimony with his signature, so we may know how our command is being carried out.

Given in our city of Grenada this 30th of the month of April, of the year of the birth of our Lord Jesus Christ Fourteen Hundred Ninety-Two. (It is marked and says: in the three said caravels during the time above mentioned).

I THE KING—I THE QUEEN

Juan de Coloma, secretary of the King and Queen, our Lord and Lady, had this written by their order. (On the back of the said decree it says as follows: "Agreed in form: Rodericus Doctor, Francisco de Madrid, Chancellor. Fees Nil." (Original).

Decree freeing from taxes all that is taken from Seville for the caravels that Christopher Columbus is taking.[12]

Santa Fe de la Vega de Grenada, 30 April 1492.
(A.G.I. Patronato 295 # 6.)

Fol.r/

The King and Queen, Landlords and tax collectors, customs officers and tithe collectors and Gate-Tax collectors, and custom men and guards and whatsoever other persons who have charge of taking and collecting whatever duties both in the very noble city of Seville, and in whatsoever other cities and towns and places in our kingdoms and seignories to each and every one of you: inasmuch as we have ordered Christopher Columbus to take certain fustas of the fleet to certain parts of the Ocean Seas on matters complying with our service, we order each and all of you to agree to and consent to take out and carry from these cities and towns and places all the victuals and maintenance and ammunition and sails rigging and other things that may be needful and the said Christopher Columbus may have brought and carried off for the said fustas without asking for or taking any fees for the same or any part of the same provided that the persons taking them swear that they are for our said fleet, and not for resale or any other purpose. Do not do otherwise under pain of our mercy and ten thousand maravedís for our exchequer.

Done at the town of Santa Fe this 30th day of the month of April of Fourteen Ninety-two years.

---

[12] Published in: Navarrete I documento No 10, pp 308-309. Co. Do. In./Am. Oc. I 38 pp 110-111.

I THE KING—I THE QUEEN

By order of the King and Queen: Juan de Coloma. (On the back of the decree reads the signature "Agreed.")
(Original).

In 1935 Emiliano Jos discovered three other documents that proved that Columbus intended to cross the Atlantic to reach Asia, the Indies, Cathay, and Cipango. [13] The first, dated 5th of May 1492 and found in the archives of Simancas, is the registration of a payment in the amount of 200,000 maravedís made to Luis de Santángel by Alonso de las Cabezas "*on account toward the sum of 400,000 maravedís needed by the Kings to equip the caravels sent to the Indies and to pay for Christopher Columbus who sails with the aforesaid fleet.*"

The second document is *The Passport* a letter issued by the Catholic Kings addressed to all rulers, first born sons and relatives of kings, dukes, marquis, captains, ship owners, officers and subjects, so that they shall facilitate in every way the voyage of Columbus. This *Passport* was signed also on the 17th of April 1492 in Granada and said "*With this letter we send the nobleman Christopher Columbus with three caravels fitted out for the oceans towards the regions of India for certain reasons and affairs concerning the propagation of the divine faith and also for our own interest and benefits . . . .*" Then the letter continues requesting from its recipients to receive well the Spanish delegation and allow free transit to " . . . . *the noblemen arriving with the caravels and other maritime vessels (vasa maritima) . . . .* " During the XV century the expression *vasa maritima* was a generalization

---

[13] Paolo Emilio Taviani: *The Great Design*, pp. 394-395. Casa Editrice De Agostini, 1992. Novara, Italy.

indicating all kinds of maritime vessels. It does not automatically mean that Columbus left with a fleet larger than he was able to equip, but it could be interpreted as an allusion to the fact that the three caravels constituted the basic ships needed for the expedition. The caravel was the most outstanding type of ship at this time to sustain an oceanic voyage. The way maritime vessels were described was very vague, unless detailed informations were given for specific purposes. Therefore the emphasis was put on *the caravel* because she was a very specific and special kind of vessel.[14]

The third document, as well as *The Passport*, was found in the *General Archive of the Crown of Aragon* in Barcelona and it is a letter of introduction from the Spanish sovereigns to the ruler of Cathay. However the name of the addressee is left out because the Kings did not know the name of the successor to the Grand Khan, who had lived there at the time of Marco Polo. The fleet's notary, Rodrigo de Escobedo, was supposed to fill in the blank space upon arrival. This letter was written on the 30th of April 1492 in Granada in triplicates and in Latin as a form of respect. In an era when the Spanish language was evolving and becoming more modern and popular, Latin was considered the language of scholars affiliated with the Church and of State officials. At any court there were plenty of men who knew Latin and could translate very easily any kind of communication written in this language.

The Spanish monarchs considered normal policy to write to the Grand Khan, or the Emperor of Japan, or any other potentate encountered during the expedition, in the language known in the courts.

---

[14] Marinella Bonvini-Mazzanti: *1492: Scoperta e conquista dell'America.* Universitá di Urbino, Studi storici, 1992. Urbino, Italy.

Letter of introduction.

"To the most serene Prince, our dearest friend: we Ferdinand and Isabella, King and Queen of Castile, Aragon, Leon, Sicily, Granada etc. send greetings and best wishes of prosperity. We know from our subjects and from others who have come here from those realms, what good will and what excellent consideration you show towards us and our state and your great desire to be informed of our happenings. We have therefore resolved to send you our noble captain Christopher Columbus, bearer of letters from which you can learn of our good health and fortune and other things that we have ordered him to tell you from us. We beg you, therefore, to have no doubts about what he and we tell you. As far as us, we would be most happy to show how ready we are to grant your wishes."

I THE KING—I THE QUEEN

From our city of Grenada, 30 April 1492. In three copies.
Secretary: Juan de Coloma.

CHAPTER 6

THE SHIPS

It is common knowledge that Columbus left the port of Palos with three caravels; however, according to the documents we have mentioned in the preceding chapter, it appears the possibility that other ships may have been part of the fleet.

The term *"caravel"* comprised all similar ships even though some had special peculiarities. The main common features were that they carried a forecastle projecting over the stern and a small poop deck aft. The main mast stood exactly amidships. The only other mast was the mizzen, which was stepped in a half deck aft of the main mast. They carried either two lateen (triangular) sails or a square mainsail or a lateen mizzen. The helmsman stood under the half deck and steered with a stern rudder, which was an innovation of this particular period, and a very long tiller.

They were the most common ships sailing the Mediterranean for trade and commercial purposes between the XIV and XVII centuries. Later the Spaniards and the Portuguese used the caravel for exploration. Before being developed for oceanic voyages, they were basically large boats without beak-head or stern-castle, having only a simple curved stem and a plain transom stern. The sails were lateen rigged on two masts (*caravela latina*).

This sail format was an inconvenience for longer oceanic voyages and so caravels were developed into three-mast ships with square rigs on the two front masts and a lateen rigged mizzens (*caravela rotunda*).

This change provided better sail-power balance and avoided lateen sail disabilities caused by the immense length of the yard on which the sail was set and the need of tacking the lower sail in order to bring the yard to the other side of the mast.

The overall average length of a three-mast caravel was 75 to 80 feet even though some were built with an overall length of 100 feet.

La Santa Maria was at this time better known in Spain as a *nao* (= Spanish word for a regular ship between the XIII and XVI centuries) and because she was Columbus' flagship and he was the captain on board, she became known as *La Nao Capitana*. She was one of the largest caravels ever built with an overall length of 95 feet. She was a three-mast square-rigged general type of cargo vessel, slow and clumsy and, according to Columbus' statements, not very well suited for voyages of exploration. She carried a crew of 40 men. According to Morison, Columbus renamed her *Santa Maria*, because her original name was "*Mariagalante*" or "*Marillega.*"

La Pinta (= the painted) was second in size. Always according to Morison, her name came from a member of the pinto family, who owned her and made it available to Columbus for the voyage. She was a three-mast square-rigged caravel approximately 70 feet in length, with a beam of about 22 feet and a draft of 7. Normally she would carry a crew of about 25 men. She was commanded by Martín Alonso Pinzón.

La Niña was the smallest of Columbus' three crafts measuring 67 feet. She was owned by Juan Niño (from whom she took her nickname meaning *"The Little Girl"*) and was built at Moguer. Originally she had been named *Santa Clara* for the city's patron saint. Juan Niño sailed as Master under the command of Vicente Yáñez Pinzón of Palos. Even though small and with lateen sails, *La Niña* proved very quickly to be seaworthy and became the admiral's favorite ship. She was one of the most advanced ships of her days. In the Canary Islands, however, to take advantage of the oceanic winds and make her even more seaworthy, Columbus changed her sails from lateen to square. When *La Santa Maria* was destroyed on Christmas Day 1492, Columbus used *La Niña* for his voyage of return and many more voyages later on.

In addition to Columbus' three famous ships documents indicate quite a few times the presence of another type of caravel called *Fusta*. This caravel had been used, before the discovery of the New World, in the Mediterranean by the Turks, the Moors, the Duke of Savoy, and the Venetians. The Portuguese began to use her in the Atlantic along the African coast by the *Ladrones de Mar*,—pirates of the sea. The main characteristic of this ship was that she had a deep cargo-hold, could carry quite a bit of weight, a crew up to forty men, and could withstand strong ocean winds because it had more than three masts and square sails. In regular times *fustas* were used for pirates' raids; in wartime they were issued letters of qualification to become part of armadas to officially validate the *Ladrones'* activities that could benefit the war. By the time Columbus was ready to undertake his expedition of discovery, apparently *fustas* had also become part of Spanish fleets to be mentioned so many times in the different documents. Nowhere, however, it is mentioned who equipped *La Fusta* or *Fustas* that followed Columbus; probably they were independent entrepreneurs or even the same *Ladrones*,[15] who needed to find other opportunities of trade and commerce once their raids' usual territories had become colonies under government regulation.

---

[15] Juan Tomas Tavares K: *Piratas de America: pp 105-108. Editora de Santo Domingo S.A., printed in Spain 1984.*

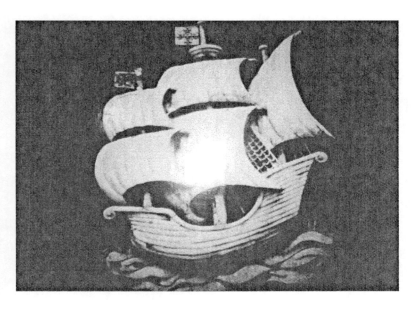

Picture of "FUSTA"
Courtesy of El Museo de Las Casas Reales
Santo Domingo

CHAPTER 7

THE CREWS

The ordinance directed to Palos' inhabitants instructed them to equip two caravels. This city's citizens had been accused and judged guilty of having offended Ferdinand and Isabella, therefore they had been fined and charged with equipping at their own expenses with provisions for one year and arming two caravels to be put at the service of the crown. The said caravels had to be remitted within ten days from the date of the ordinance to Christopher Columbus, who at the same time was equipping *La Santa Maria* on his own.

The notary Francisco Fernández read this ordinance on May 23, 1492, in the church of St. George in Palos in the presence of civil authorities and Father Juan Pérez, who had been very important in Columbus' life and very influential in convincing the monarchs to undertake this enterprise. This ordinance was quite a shock for the city officials also because the monarchs were not giving a clear explanation of the events to come.

Trusting completely a foreigner to cross an ocean to accomplish such a mission for Spain was too much to ask from expert sailors who were foreseeing their lives and their vessels put in grave danger. But Columbus as well as the sovereigns had already considered such reaction, since another ordinance, which allowed the suspension of all criminal and civil cases in favor of whoever would embark, accompanied the first.

The admiral was foreseeing the probable difficulties he would encounter in outfitting the fleet especially because all details had to remain secret. He also knew that in Palos he was going to encounter even more difficulties because the authorities on experienced navigation were the Pinzón brothers.

Columbus had already met Martín Alonso Pinzón about his project and had found him favorable to the possibility of collaboration. But after this meeting Columbus changed his mind and decided to organize the expedition on his own, even if it meant to include in the crew criminals and face the hostility of Pinzón. Probably this change was due to the fact that the documents about his titles and honors were uncertain, or in other words, not completely legal until the discovery had taken place.

Columbus at this point did not want to lose any earned merit or honor by sharing them with others. He was a foreigner and in case the Pinzón brothers, being Spanish, had returned from the expedition ahead of him to announce the new discoveries, they would be recognized as the discoverers and Columbus would be forgotten.

By mid-June the inhabitants of Palos had not yet executed the order therefore the Crown recalled them. It became clear at this time that until Columbus had reached an agreement with the Pinzón brothers, nobody was going to undertake the outfitting of the caravels. The convicts were only four and the crews were formed of expert sailors.

La Santa Maria had 40 men, of which 39 are listed in Columbus' log; *La Pinta* had 26 seamen; *La Niña* 22 seamen.

A captain commanded every ship, however in the case of *La Santa Maria,* whose master and owner was Juan de la Cosa, Columbus was the admiral of the fleet and the commander on board.

Vicente Yáñez Pinzón was captain of *La Niña* until Columbus took over after *La Santa Maria* was shipwrecked. Historians have always disputed the role of the Pinzón brothers in this voyage of discovery. Their participation was decisive in convincing the sailors of Palos, Huelva, and Moguer to overcome the fear of the *"Dark Sea."*

The most important personality on board was the pilot, who was responsible for keeping the course. He could read maps, use all instruments of navigation, and many times he was the sole expert in knowing the action of the tides. On *La Santa Maria,* Columbus, because of the experience acquired in the early years of his life in Portugal, was the only other person capable of overseeing the pilot's functions.

Others with significant tasks included the boatswain, who was lieutenant to the master or captain and was in charge of carrying on their orders distributing the work among the men, setting sail, and doing general cleaning and maintenance.

The notary was basically a recorder of the possession—taking of the discovered lands and the loading and unloading to and from the vessels.

The marshal was in charge of rationing the potable water and could assume authority of judge in disputes, quarrels, and even crimes with power of punishing and condemning.

The comptroller kept account of expenses and was responsible for the crown's share of gold.

The steward rationed the food and the wine. He oversaw the trimming of the lamps, the building of fires, and the turning over of the sandglasses.

The other tradesmen in the crew were all performing individual tasks according to their trades. The masters and pilots received 20,000 maravedís per month, the expert sailors 1,000, and the ship-boys 666.

The condemned men who enjoyed the royal pardon for participating in this voyage of discovery were only four: Bartolomé Torres, who had been condemned to death for killing a man in a quarrel. The other three—Alonso Clavijo, Juan de Moguer, and Pedro Yzquierdo de Lepe—were guilty of organizing an escape from jail.

The three crews were mostly formed of Spaniards, except for five exceptions: Columbus and ship-boy Jacomo el Rico from Genoa; ship-boy Juan Arias from Portugal; seaman Antonio Calabrese from Calabria; and seaman Giovanni Vecano from Venice. Among the Spaniards one was from Murcia, 10 from Galicia and the pays Basque, and the remaining 70 were from Andalusia.

Martín and Vicente Pinzón brought with them a younger brother, the Niños were father and son, the Quinteros were two brothers, the Perézes were uncle and nephew, the Arráezes were father and son, and the Medeles two brothers.[16]

---

[16] *Paolo Emilio Taviani: Christoforo Colombo pp. 125-127. Casa Editrice de Agostini, 1992, Novara, Italy.*

CHAPTER 8

LIFE ABOARD A CARAVEL

Susceptible to the sea's merciless forces and utterly depending upon the winds, sailors, during the age of the caravels, took comfort in religious ceremonies. The officers who stood watch on the high rear deck placed the images of the saints along the rails to give them solace. This practice led to the term poop deck from the Latin word *"Pupa"* (= doll).

On a typical day dawn was announced by a cabin boy chanting a blessing, then the *Pater Noster* and the *Ave Maria* was recited on deck by the sailors. When the seventh hourglass was turned over (ca. 6:30 a.m.) the cabin boy was wishing everyone a good day with another chant. By the next turn of the hourglass it was 7:00 a.m. and the beginning of the workday.

Before beginning of the first night watch, a boatswain put out the fire and at the turning of the next hourglass, indicating the beginning of the night watch, he wished good night to everyone with another chant.

The sailors' daily routine included mopping the bridge, braiding oakum, mending sails, pumping the bilge, and doing different chores subdivided into watches.

This daily routine was modified on Saturday with the singing of the *Salve Regina* and the reciting of the litanies. After such recitations the master invited everyone to recite the *Apostolic Creed*.

Bureaucracy was also a very important part of life on-board. Historians have called Spain *"The Paper Empire"* because of the enormous record keeping and attention for details. Everything was recorded in several copies even when at sea in the cabins of the officials.

The lodging on a regular size caravel was the following: the officers slept on pallets over mats below the deck near the rudder. The master, the pilot, and perhaps the marshal or the notary had small separate apartments away from the hold. The seamen slept in a corner of the deck or castle. They were forbidden to sleep in the hold so as to be able to respond promptly to emergencies.

On *La Santa Maria* the lodgings were completely different. After the ship had been built and equipped for the expedition, at least one third of the deck was modified to lodge the admiral in dignity. The cabin reserved for him was very simply furnished: it had a table, a chair, a stool, a trunk, a strongbox, writing material and tableware, wash basin, and canopy bed.

The walls were decorated with motifs such as shields, armors, swords, navigational instruments, the flags of Castile and Léon, and the image of our Lady of Guadalupe, to whom Columbus was very devoted.

La Santa Maria had a large crew and the state of discipline used in the other caravels could not be maintained in the same manner. Personal effects were kept in community chests of different sizes according to the different ranks. The discovery of hammocks used by the Tainos Indians solved the sleeping problems for the sailors on large ships.

The food that was provided for a full year was water, wine, oil, vinegar, salt, flour, hardtack, lard, pork fat, lentils, onions, fava beans, garlic, olives, dried fish and dried meat, rice, sugar, jams, honey, cheese, almonds, raisins and other dried fruit. During the stop in Gomera, in the Canary Islands, were added livestock (goats). They were fed dried grass and killed sporadically during the voyage to provide fresh meat.

Lunch was served at 11:00 a.m. before the changing of the watch. The officers ate at a table unlike the seamen who collected their food near the stove holding their bowls and handing them to the servants to be filled; then they ate while sitting on the floor in the most comfortable place they could find.

The sailors did not wear uniforms. The casual outfit was a cape with hood, breeches, and a conical red cap. The heralds wore red breeches, a vest with mandarin sleeves with the coat of arms of Spain embroidered on the breast, and also a red cap made out of plain cotton cloth instead of wool. These quasi-uniforms were made in Toledo and probably Columbus had more than the crew could use because he gave some to the Indians. Columbus most of the time wore a red outfit and a gray cape that was made by Franciscan monks.[17]

---

[17] Opus cited on #16 page 67.

CHAPTER 9

THE INSTRUMENTS

When Columbus undertook his voyage trying to find a way across the unmarked ocean it was more a matter of art than science. Sailors of the Middle Ages followed the movements of the stars and the direction of the wind. When the compass was invented it became possible to sail an unknown sea without fear of the fog and of the clouds hiding the stars, especially Polaris. Navigating along the coast was not always necessary to rely on instruments because land was always in sight. But when ships began to attack the open ocean, more complex and precise instruments would be needed. Still, even with instruments, sailing directions and charts, ships were frequently off course.

The latitude could be calculated fairly accurately, but the longitude was another story. Without a precise time-keeping device (chronometer) a ship's position East-West of the principal meridian was just too difficult to determine. When landfall was anticipated, the ship spent the night anchored to avoid running aground. The astrolabe had been so far the main navigation instrument. With it navigators could measure the angle of the sun or of the polar star from the horizon.

The compass indicated the ship's course; her position could be estimated by measuring the speed and the course, and within sight of land certain familiar points could also identify her position. In uncharted and unfamiliar waters the depth of the waters was measured with a *"sounding lead"* (aplomb) known as *"dipsey"* or *"deep sea lead."*

The invention of the mariner's compass was the most important invention to solve all problems. With this instrument became possible to know the direction of the North and relate to it the scuttle of the ship.

From a maritime point of view the discovery of America was the result of advancement of mathematical calculations and perfection of instruments such as the compass with the magnetic needle, the forestaff, the astrolabe, and the portable sundial. All these factors made possible Columbus' voyage.

The *"Urca"* (= hooker, dogger) used by Spain in the Mediterranean was a derivation of the old Roman *"vasa maritima"* to which succeeded the caravel for Atlantic voyages because it comprised a keel, a lateen sail, and a movable helm. After Columbus the modification of *La Santa Maria* from caravel to *nao* inspired the creation of new ships like frigates and galleons.

From a social point of view this discovery was a demographic expansion supported by the Renaissance man's spirit of adventure. Religiously speaking the possibility of evangelization was giving the church even more universal power. Finally for the nation's economy the finding of new routes to the Indies was fulfilling the European need for precious metals and spices.[18]

---

[18] Information taken from exhibits panels at the Maritime Museum in Santo Domingo, Dominican Republic. *January 17, 2004.*

CHAPTER 10

THE STOP AT GOMERA

When Columbus sailed from Palos on August 3, 1492, he had already planned to stop in Gomera, in the Canary Islands before beginning the crossing of the ocean, because he wanted the help of Beatriz de Bobadilla, Governor of the island. He had met Beatriz at the Spanish court when she was a young girl and favorite of Ferdinand. Her cousin, the marquise of Moya and her husband, Andrés de Cabrera, had been a great influence in convincing the queen to understand Columbus' genius and to support his project. Columbus considered them among the group of his court protectors.

Beatriz had been ordered by Isabella to marry Hernán de Peraza, Governor of Gomera, and leave immediately after the wedding. In November of 1488 Hernán was killed by a gang of Guanches (= Gomera natives), who could no longer endure his tyranny.[19]

---

[19] Paolo Emilio Taviani: *"The Grand Design" p. 483 and "The Great Discovery"* pp. 30-40. *Casa Editrice de Agostini, 1992. Novara, Italy.*

According to Spanish legend the name Gomera was taken from Gomer, Noah's grandson, whose offsprings, the Gomerans, populated the island after the Great Flood.

Because of the fertility of this land, Columbus had chosen to stop here to supply the ships with grains, vegetables, and fruit that were growing all year through. But there was also another reason. Columbus wanted to start the crossing on the same parallel as the island of Hierro, the same island mentioned in the map drawn by the captain, who had died in his house.

In 1492 all conflicts with Portugal over the ownership of the Canary Islands had ended. The Treaty of Alcaçobas in 1479 and The Peace of Toledo in 1480 had been confirmed by Pope Sixtus IV in his bull "*Aeterni Regis*" in 1481 giving Spain complete ownership of the Canary Islands. However in 1492 the Guanches still occupied Tenerife and La Palma islands. In other words, Spain's sovereignty had been assured only on the other islands of the archipelagos.

After her husband's death, Beatriz de Peranza became Governor of Gomera and more interested in affairs of state than in her family.

"On the 9th of August La Pinta reached the Grand Canary in the morning and I ordered Martín Alonso to remain here until the caravel could be properly repaired and the rudder replaced. I took La Santa Maria and La Niña and set to Gomera."

During Columbus' stay in Gomera from August 12 to September 6, some historians said that he was "touched by love" for Doña Beatriz. It is certain, however, that she helped him with the provisions and provided food and accommodations for him in her house.

Here in Gomera Columbus needed her help in converting the sails of *La Niña* from lateen to square to make her even more shifty and responsive to the ocean winds. So Beatriz found "many noble Spaniards"—a fact that surprised Columbus—willing to help. Even though the Canary Islands were also known as *"The Fortunate Isles,"* they were a poor country and the only known society was the native Guanches. However this matter was later clarified by the fact that, after studies on the Guanches Society, it was discovered that from the time the Canaries became a Spanish possession, the Guanches had submitted to the crown of Castile and adopted Catholicism and the Castilian language. So even though without riches generated by gold, silver, and precious metals some of the Guanches became nobility because of the amount of land and livestock they owned.

Title page of "History of Canary Islands."

CHAPTER 11

THE LETTER TO SANTÁNGEL

On March 4, 1493 Columbus had returned from his voyage of discovery. Exactly seven months and one day had gone by after the departure from Palos. The admiral had come back on board of *La Niña* and landed in Lisbon. He was very anxious to let the sovereigns know about his discoveries also because he had lost sight of *La Pinta*, commanded by Martín Alonso Pinzón already docked at Baiona, a small port on the northeast coast of Spain, and feared that the brothers Pinzón would claim the right of discovery. Columbus arrived to Palos on March 15 and *La Pinta* arrived on the same day a few hours after Columbus.

By the time Columbus had made a short stop at the Azores Islands he had already prepared *Las Relaciones*, a report to be sent to all the influential personalities at court. But the report to Luis de Santángel remains the most important and famous for being more detailed than all the others.

Columbus wrote:

"*My Lord, because I know that you will have pleasure in knowing about the great victory that God has granted me during this voyage, I write to you this letter in which you will learn how in thirty-four days I have gone from the Canary Islands to the Indies, with the fleet that the illustrious king and queen have given me. Here I have found a great number of islands, populated by many inhabitants, of which I have taken possession in the name of their Highnesses with legal proclamation and royal flags without encountering opposition. To the first islands by me discovered I have given the name of San Salvador, in honor of the omnipotent God who has created so many marvels. The Indians call it "Guanahani." I gave to the second island the name of "Santa Maria de la Conceptión and to the third the name of "Fernandina." I called the fourth "Isabela" and the fifth "Juana" and many different other names to all the ones I have discovered.*[20] *When I arrived to Juana, I sailed along the west side of the coast and I found it so large that I thought it was part of Cathai. But because I could not find any villages, except for a couple of fisherman's huts inhabited by a few men, who began to flee as soon as they spotted us, we continued to sail hoping to find a village or a city soon. After having gone quite a few leagues and noticed that the coast was offering no possibilities, against my will and because winter was approaching and winds were also against us, I kept sailing north to go back to a port I had already spotted and sent two men on land to discover whether there were large cities nearby. After a three-day-march they found many villages with plenty of inhabitants who had no government and so they came back to the ship. Finally, from some Indians I had captured, I was able to understand*

---

[20] Santa María de la Conceptión is today Rum Cay, Fernandina is Long island, Isabela is formed by two islands called Crooked and Fortune separated by a strait in which is found a third islet called Bird Rock. Juana is today's Cuba.

that the land was an island and I decided to sail around its coast toward east for a length of one-hundred-seven leagues up to the place where it was forming a promontory.[21]

On the east of this cape, 18 leagues from the first island, I found another island that I called Española. I directed the ship toward it and sailed along the coast on the north side for a length of one hundred eighty-eight leagues as I did along the coast of Juana. This isle, as well as the others, is very fertile. It has infinity of natural ports, which cannot be compared to any others in the Christian lands for beauty and location and many rivers just marvelous to look at. The configuration of this Hispañola is exceptional: there are very high mountain chains much higher than in Tenerife. They are simply majestic and various. All of them are accessible and covered with trees so tall that seem to touch the sky. It seems to me that these trees do not lose their leaves because I have always seen them green and as beautiful as the trees in Spain during the month of May. Some were even in bloom; some had fruits. I could hear the birds singing in a thousand different ways wherever I was going even though it was November. There are six or eight different species of palm trees and I am ecstatic to look at all these varieties of plants. There are marvelous pine forests and fields: there is honey, many species of birds and fruits never seen before. Inland there are mines and quite a few inhabitants. Hispañola is stupendous: the mountains, the valleys, the plains are so fertile that anything can be planted, cattle can be raised and cities and villages can be built. The ports on the ocean are of extreme beauty; the rivers are many and quite large with pure waters that in many cases carry gold. Here the vegetation is different than in the Juana where there are many types of spices and mines of gold and different other metals.

---

[21] At this point Columbus thought to have reached Cathay according to the description of the land given by Marco Polo, but not having found the city of Cipango he realized he had failed.

The inhabitants of this island, as the ones of all the others, are naked even though some of the women cover the superior parts of their bodies with tree leaves or with a piece of cloth woven especially for this purpose. They do not use iron or steel to make arms because they are shy. The only arms they know are made out of bamboo picked after the blooming season on which extremities they attach a piece of wood very pointy. Many times they do not even use this weapon. In fact I was able to drag to the ground two or three men who were approaching to speak with us and the ones, who were coming to protect them, fled as soon as they saw this happen. No harm had been done to any of them because everywhere I have gone I have brought presents with me without receiving anything in return. They are so shy that it is not possible to approach them, but once they have been reassured that no harm is done to them they are so generous and hospitable that nobody can believe it unless they see it with their own eyes. They never refuse what is demanded of them and, when in possession of an object wanted by us, they cannot wait to give it with great friendship. They are always very happy no matter how cheap is the object they receive in exchange. I had to forbid my men to give them objects of no value like broken dishes, pieces of glass, strips of ribbon even though they think that these items are precious. It happened that one of the sailors received a gold nugget valued at two and a half "Castellanos"[22] for just a piece of colorful ribbon and many other sailors received also much more than what they had exchanged was worth. Many times for a new "Blanca"[23] these Indians gave all they owned up to the value of two or more "Castellanos" or one or more "Arroba"[24] of cotton thread. The sailors were exchanging anything they could find including pieces of broken kegs and pieces of scrap metal like real animals to the point that I had to stop this dishonest trading. I gave to these native many of my valuable objects that I had brought with me for the purpose of making them friends and convert them to Christianity; to make them love Their Highnesses and the

---

[22] Ancient Spanish Coin.
[23] Old Spanish copper coin.
[24] Unit of weight equivalent to 25lbs. or 11.5 kgs.

whole Castilian nation so they could procure and remit to us the products that they have in abundance and we need so much.

These Indians do not profess any particular kind of religion nor they know idolatry. They believe that every power and every goodness comes from the sky: they also believe that even I with my ships and my men have come from the sky and because of such belief they have received us in a friendly manner after their first fears had gone. Such sentiments do not stem from ignorance. These Indians are very intelligent; they can navigate the seas and explain everything in a terrific manner, but they have never seen our kinds of ships nor men dressed in clothes. As soon as we landed on the first island I took some by force to have them tell me everything that could be found on it and so it happened that quite fast we were able to understand each other in words and gestures. This way these men have rendered great service. I am holding them with me even now and they still believe that I have come from the sky. Wherever we land they want to be the first to announce the news going from house to house screaming "come to see the men from the sky." Men, women, and children, after having been reassured that it was safe to meet us, came to bring us food and drinks with incredible amiability.

They have in all islands canoes with oars made like our fustas, some smaller, some longer, and some even longer than a fusta with eighteen benches, but not very large because they are carved out of a single tree trunk, and extremely fast to outdo our fustas. With these crafts they go from island to island to transport their merchandise. I have seen enter in one from sixty to eighty men, each one at one oar.[25] *In these islands I have not noticed a difference*

---

[25] Marinella Bonvini Mazzanti: "1492: *Scoperta e Conquista dell'America.*" Columbus by using the word "fusta" knew exactly what kind of vessel he was describing. This vessel was also made from a single tree trunk with benches for eighteen to thirty men. A "fusta" with lateen or square sails could certainly go faster than the one with oars, therefore could be used for oceanic voyages.

in their customs nor in their language—they all understand each other. I hope that Their Highnesses will take care of their conversion to the Christian faith to which they seem to be very inclined.

I have already explained how I have navigated 107 leagues along the coast of Juana from west to east and basing my knowledge on this experience I can say that Juana is larger than England and Scotland together, because, besides the 107 leagues, on the west side there are still two provinces to be yet explored, one of which is called "Avan" where the people have tails. These two provinces must be at least another 50 or 60 leagues away from here, according to what I have learned from the Indians still with me who know all these isles. Española measures in perimeter more than Spain following the coast from Colliure to Fuentarrabìa in the Gulf of Guascogne, because in sailing only around one side from west to east, I have covered a distance of 188 great leagues. This place is a dreamland and, after having seen it once, it is difficult to forget it. Even though I have taken possession of all the other islands—that are richer than expected—in the names of Their Highnesses so they can dispose as they please for the benefit of Spain, this island Hispañola, I say, is the best place to exploit for its gold mines. To start commerce between the two continents, I have taken possession of a great village called "Village Navidad" where I have begun to build a fenced-in fort that should be finished by now. Here I have left a sufficient number of men with arms, artillery, provision for a year, and the fusta[26] with the master Mariner and other tradesmen to become friends with the king of the land. This king felt very honored to consider us brothers and, even if he would change his mind, his subjects, not used to arms or armors, being always naked, can easily be destroyed with the amount of ammunitions I have left for this purpose. It is an island where our men will not incur in any kind of danger as long as

---

[26] Marinella Bonvini Mazzanti: *"1492: Scoperta e Conquista dell'America."* This admission of having left "the fusta" at Fort Navidad indicates with certainty that Columbus had in the fleet at least four ships.

they know how to behave themselves. In all these islands it seems that the men are happy with only one wife, while the Chief or King can have up to twenty. The women work more than the men. I have not been able to find out whether they own personal property. It seems that everything is commonly owned, especially the food.

In these islands I have not found monstrous men as commonly believed. They all have an agreeable appearance and they are not black like the inhabitants of Guinea, except that they have long and affluent hair, which does not grow where the body is most exposed to the powerful sunrays. The sun here is very strong because we are only 26 degrees away from the equator, but where there are mountains the winter cold is very pungent. The natives are tolerating this cold by ingesting spicy food.

We have not yet seen any monsters. There is only one island, the second at the entrance to the Indies, where the population is believed to be very fierce and eating human flesh. These natives possess many canoes to raid the other islands, rob, and kill as much as they can. They are not less handsome than the others, but they wear their hair long and tied in a ponytail like the women. They use bows and arrows made from pointed pieces of wood for lack of iron. They are ferocious compared to the other populations, but I do not consider them more dangerous than any others. These are the ones who have rapports with the women of "Matinino" the first island encountered coming from Spain, because there are no men there. These women do not occupy themselves with feminine duties, but know how to use bows and arrows and they protect their bodies with a sheet of copper, a very abundant metal in the island.

I have also learned that there is another island even bigger than Hispañola where the people have no hair in any part of their body. In this island there is much gold and I am bringing with me some men from it as witnesses. In conclusion, Their Highnesses will see that what has been accomplished from this voyage is the fact that I can give them all the gold they need if they will help me. Even more spices, cotton, gum mastic, of the quality that up to today has been only found in the isle of Chio in Greece

that can be sold at a very high price, aloe wood, and slaves chosen from idolaters. I also think to have found rhubarb and cinnamon and I will find even more precious merchandise thanks to the persons I have left there. When the winds were propitious I kept on sailing and did not stop in any particular port to investigate, except for the Village Navidad where I landed and paused to leave everything in order. I could have accomplished even more if the vessels had been more apt to my needs. Most of this enterprise should not be attributed to the genius and industry of the human race, but to the intercession of God, who grants victory to everyone who relies on his help in impossible enterprises. And ours was certainly one of those. Everything was based on conjectures not proven by experience, and everyone who was listening knew that this whole project could have been only an illusion. So it was the powerful hand of the Redeemer that gave this victory to our illustrious king and queen and their realms, which will become famous. The Christian community should rejoice with great feasts and thank the Holy Trinity with prayers for the increment that it will receive from the conversion of all these peoples to our faith as well as from the earthly goods from which not only Spain, but also the whole world can benefit. I am reporting in a very brief manner everything that has been accomplished. Written on board of La Niña near the Canary Islands the 15th of February 1493.
The Admiral."

"After having written this letter and still on board of my ship in the Sea of Castile I was attacked by such strong winds that I had to lighten it. Today I have stopped at the port of Lisbon, from where I have decided to write to Their Highnesses, to make repairs generating great astonishment. In all the Indies I have witnessed storms like the ones in Spain during the month of May. I went there in 33 days and came back in 28. In this sea here, however, these tempests have retarded my arrival of 14 days. All seamen say that the winter has been very severe and there have never been so many shipwrecks.
Written on the 4th of March 1493."

This letter is very important because it has reached us as it was originally written, without the kind of manipulation in transcription or translation, as sometimes happens with copies. It can also be considered an official document because it is written as a report (= Relación) to an important personality at court with the intention to make it public. It acquired also the value of a legal document.

Columbus showing a coin to a Taino Indian
Oil on canvas from Juan Medina Ramirez
Santo Domingo

CHAPTER 12

THE RETURN

At his arrival in Lisbon, Columbus went to visit King John II of Portugal with the six Indians he had brought with him from the West Indies. When the king realized that they were not the same types as the ones in Guinea at the Fort La Mina, he was very pleased, but at the same time he regretted not having sponsored the expedition and tried to impede Columbus to reach Spain. Columbus did not feel any longer secure waiting in Portugal and on March 13, 1493 he sailed for Palos. In Palos he stayed with Martín Alonso Pinzón at La Rábida monastery until he received news from King Ferdinand on April 7 that he would be received in Barcelona. From Palos he traveled over land to Seville and then to Barcelona.

Bartolomé de Las Casas in his *"Historia de las Indias"* describes Columbus' reception by the sovereigns as an apotheosis, a terrific grand celebration.

"The people swarmed in the streets all marveling at the sight of this venerable personality who, it is said, had discovered another

world and at the sight of the Indians, parrots, objects, gems, and the golden jewelry he bore, which they had never seen before."

Many great noblemen from Castile, Cataluña, Valencia, and Aragon, all most anxious to see the arrival of the one who had completed an undertaking so grand that caused rejoicing throughout the Christian world, were waiting with the Sovereigns. Columbus entered the room where the monarchs were, accompanied by a multitude of knights and nobles. He stood among them like a Roman Senator because of his authoritative stature, his venerable head of gray hair and a modest smile, which increased the pleasure and glory with which he greeted. After kissing the monarchs' hands and giving a detailed account of the voyage, Columbus presented the Sovereigns with the new subjects and offered them the riches of the newly discovered lands. The ceremony ended with a solemn "Te Deum" intoned by the cantors of the Royal Chapel while the monarchs knelt and the whole court wept for joy with their hearts filled with thankfulness for the beautiful and numerous gifts."

All the documents drawn in April 1492 assume now a difference value and with this happy return everything has changed and all doubts have vanished. All conditions had been fulfilled. As a reward the monarchs allowed Columbus to add to his coat of arms the gold castle of Castile and the purple lion of León. On May 28, 1493 in Barcelona the admiral was named Captain General of the second fleet to depart for the Indies.

While in Barcelona, Columbus wrote letters to his supporters and at the same time he sent *"La Relación"*(= his report) to Pope Alexander VI as basis for the preparation of the bull *"Inter caetera . . ."* regarding the Spanish jurisdiction in the new lands. Also he sent to his friend Gabriel Sánchez the same letter he had sent to Luis de Santángel describing the customs of the Indians, their amiability, the natural beauty of the islands, the possibility of finding plenty of gold, spices, precious woods, and finally the construction of *La Navidad* where he left *La Fusta* with the 39 men. This letter was translated into

Latin by Leandro Cosco, a Spanish employee at the Vatican, in April 1493 and sent to all the European nations. Cosco translated the word *fusta* as "*item quondam caravellam.*" Being a Catalan, Cosco knew the difference between the types of sea vessels used by Spain and also knew that *La Fusta* was a pirate ship used in raids. So he changed it to caravel thinking that this word would be more appropriate to emphasize the expedition's spirit of evangelization.[27]

There was also the hypothesis that *La Fusta* could have been already changed into a caravel in Gomera before Columbus' departure. This second hypothesis is confirmed in the letter of Annibale de Gennaro, special papal envoy to Barcelona, to his brother Antonio reporting that the news at court was that Columbus had accomplished his enterprise with "four ships."[28] Also, by the time the letter to Sánchez had been translated into Latin and sent all over Europe, everyone in Spain knew from Santángel that Columbus had left *La Fusta* at *La Navidad* in Española.

On January 2, 1493, two days before the departure from Española, Columbus wrote in his Log:

"*I left in this island, that the Indians call Bohío, 39 men in the fortress under the command of three officers, all of whom have become very friendly with King Guacanagari. In command is Don Diego de Arana, a native of Córdova, whom I have given all of the powers I have received from the Sovereigns in full. Next in line, if something should happen to him, is his lieutenant Pedro Gutiérrez, the representative of the Royal Household. Next in line of succession is the lieutenant Rodrigo de Escobedo, Secretary of the fleet and native of Segovia, nephew of friar Rodrigo Pérez. I also left persons qualified in construction among which Alonso*

---

[27] Marinella Bonvini Mazzanti: "1492: Scoperta e Conquista dell'America."

[28] "Fondo Estense Potenze Estere" *Milano*. Exemplum Litterarum *of Ascanio Sforza to Ludovico il Moro.*

Morales, carpenter; Lope, joiner; Diego Pérez, painter; Chachú, boatswain; Juan de Medina, tailor; Domingo Vizcaino, cooper; Maestre Alonso and Maestre Juan, surgeons."

The fact that two surgeons were left at *La Navidad* further proves that Columbus had four ships. It was a basic rule of navigation that every ship had to have a doctor on board and Columbus would not have attempted such a voyage without the proper number of physicians. He returned with Maestre Diego in *La Pinta* and Maestre Alonso from Moguer in *La Niña*.

Columbus received at Court
Painting by Ricardo Balaca
National Museum of History, Buenos Aires.

Top left stored at La Rábida, Palos.
Top right stored in Palazzo Municipale, Genoa.
Center stored in House of Trade with the Indies, Seville.

CHAPTER 13

ANNIBALE DE GENNARO'S LETTER

In 1493 when the exultant news of Columbus' discovery became known, the interests of the European nations switched to the forming of political alliances. From this *"modus operandi"* arose the necessity for the various princes to be informed by diplomatic sources accredited to the different courts. The ambassadors had the duty to send the minutest details about the changes happening at court so their lords would know what to do.

Annibale de Gennaro was in Spain in April 1493, as a special envoy from the Vatican, and had been asked by his brother Antonio, who was the spokesperson for the King of Naples in Milan, to keep him informed about the current Spanish events.

The de Gennaro family had been in the diplomatic service of the King of Naples, Don Ferrante of Aragon, King Ferdinand's brother, for many years. Annibale was a cultured person who had traveled extensively; his signature on legal documents was always in Latin, *Hannibal Januarius*, to make everyone understand how he was sensitive to the humanistic culture and was trying to translate the humanities into the practices of a natural normal daily life. Being at the court of Spain as a special papal envoy he could have had access to certain information, which even though not secret, at least was reserved for the eyes and ears of a selected few. His letter reads: [29]

"Honored brother,
This day I am writing to you before any other messenger receives the order to write to you. The month of August of the past year has seen this king, at the request of a certain Columbus, issue an edict to arm and equip ***four caravels*** *for him to navigate the ocean in a direct route to the West, being the world round and so bound to find the Orient. And so he did as soon as the mentioned caravels were ready. He took the route to the West through the Strait*[30] *and, from the letters he has written which I have seen, he arrived in 34 days to a great island in which lived human beings with red skin, naked, shy, and without bellicose intent. Some of the men went ashore to find information and learn their language so they could communicate with them. As soon as they were no longer afraid, being quite intelligent, they were making themselves understood through signs and other ways so our men found that they were in the islands of the Indies. These Indians went to their nearest villages to announce that a man sent from God had landed and had met with him in good faith to offer friendship and love. When our men continued their route, after having left this island, they found a quantity of isles among them one larger than England and Scotland together and another larger than Spain. He has left there some men with provisions and ammunitions after having started the construction of a fortress. He came back with six natives so*

---

[29] Translation from the original in medieval Italian. Boldness added.
[30] The strait of Gibraltar known at this time as the Columns of Hercules.

they could learn our language. In these islands he has found pepper, wood, aloe, and gold in many rivers—in other words many rivers carry in their sand gold particles. The men over there navigate in canoes whose largest can hold from seventy to eighty rowers. Columbus has returned and landed in Lisbon. As soon as he landed, he wrote to the monarchs who have ordered him to return immediately to Spain. I hope to be able to see the letter that he has written to the sovereigns so I can send you a copy. And, after he has arrived here, anything else that the letter does not say that I might hear at court. In this court it is now known that the Indians do not have any type of government, nor do they belong to a sect; they believe that anything comes from the creator and it should be easy to convert them to the Christian faith. Columbus also says that he was in a province where men have tails. Don Diego Lopez de Aro will leave tomorrow. He is going to speak in Rome to offer the services of the Spanish sovereigns to Pope Alexander VI, as I have already written to you. He brings with him 60 mules, 20 carriages and plenty of silver: from Rome he will go to Naples. There is nothing else worthy of mention.

Barcelona 19th of March 1493
Your obedient brother Hannibal Januarius.

We need to notice that de Gennaro wrote "***four caravels***" very clearly in words and not in numbers, indicating so that *La nao capitana (La Santa Maria)* as well as *La fusta* had become two new types of vessels in this expedition.

A letter of Don Luis de la Cerda Duke of Medinaceli, who had offered hospitality to Columbus many times during his stay in Spain, mentions that, from the very first day, he had been convinced about the validity of Columbus plan and had offered to put at the stranger's disposal ***"four caravels"*** of his own fleet. However when he went to court to make this proposal to Ferdinand and Isabella he received a refusal because the sovereigns had in their minds that the realization of the enterprise should be automatically the duty of the crown.

On March 19, 1493, the Duke Medinaceli went to see Cardinal Pedro Gonzáles de Mendoza—who could corroborate his testimony—to remind him of the offer he had made to the monarchs and how he had interceded for Columbus. This time however he wanted to ask the queen for her consent to send to the new lands "*algunas caravelas*" (= some caravels) of his fleet on a yearly basis.

The Duke Medinaceli was the richest feudal lord in Spain and by asking to be the first to travel to the new lands was giving the Spanish crown a great success. Columbus' first voyage had been accomplished mostly under the auspices of the court of Castile, whose authority was only Queen Isabella, before the political union of the two kingdoms had happened.

CHAPTER 14

POPE ALEXANDER VI'S BULLS

The Spanish ambassador had left in haste to bring the pope the news of Columbus' success. It was believed all over Europe that the division of the new lands would be favorable for Spain because Pope Alexander VI was Spanish. But at this time Pope Alexander VI and Ferdinand were not on the best of terms.

When Alexander VI had become pope, he nominated his son Cesare Borgia as the Archbishop of Valencia and Valdona. The Spanish kings had not given their consent to this nomination because Alexander VI's politics were very hostile to Ferdinand of Aragon, King of Naples and cousin of Ferdinand of Spain.

The Neapolitan Ferdinand was the son of Alfonso the Magnanimous, King of Aragon and Naples, who, at his death, had divided his realm between his natural son Ferdinand to whom he gave the Kingdom of Naples, and his brother Juan II to whom he had given Aragon, Sicily and Sardinia. With Juan II's death Ferdinand became king of Aragon and of the two Sicilies. Very strict family ties existed between the two Ferdinands.

Alexander VI had been elected pope thanks to the maneuvers of Ascanio Sforza, brother of Ludovico il Moro, Duke of Milan, and conducted a politics similar to the Milanese duke in favor of Charles VIII, King of France, instead of Spain.

On May 22, 1492 Cardinal Ascanio wrote to his brother Ludovico: ".... *Yesterday two letters arrived from Spain to our Lord which were announcing good things for our Holiness and, among others, the king and queen have demonstrated good intentions toward our Holiness by allowing his son to receive the Archbishopric of Valencia and Valdona, because it was time to do things the way His Holiness wanted . . .* "

However even in 1493, after Columbus' discovery, some hostilities existed still and the Spanish kings reminded the papal ambassador " . . . *the interfering in matters concerning His Grace was interfering in their own.* "

Amicable rapports between the pontiff and the Spanish crown were reestablished after the marriage of the second son of the pope, Giovanni Borgia Duke of Gandía, who married the daughter of Ferdinand's uncle María Enríquez.

Alexander VI issued the bull *"Inter Caetera"* concerning the division of the new lands on May 3, 1493, which had to be annulled for a new *"Inter Caetera"* that was issued the day after and made public during the month of June. The third bull *"Eximiae devotionis"* was made public in July 1493.

The first bull had not clearly defined the demarcation line between the possessions of Spain and Portugal; therefore a second was needed to remedy the omissions of the first. The third finally resulted in uniting the spiritual privileges mentioned in the first and in limiting the demarcation line established in the second. The bull *"Inter caetera"* of May 4 remains the most important because it was defining *"La Raya"*—the line of demarcation between the possessions of Spain and the ones of Portugal one hundred leagues west of the Azores Islands tracing a straight route from the Arctic to the Antarctic pole.

Alexander VI's bulls confirm what Pope Nicholas V had already started in the one entitled *"Romanus Pontifex"* of January 8, 1455 about the Portuguese colonization of Africa with the words "... *so that the barbaric populations be conquered and converted to Christianity* . . ." charging this way Spain with the moral principal of evangelization.

The contents of Alexander VI's bulls were based upon the information sent by the Spanish monarchs as well as Columbus himself emphasizing the construction of *La Navidad* and the chosen men left there to continue the exploration and to convert the natives.

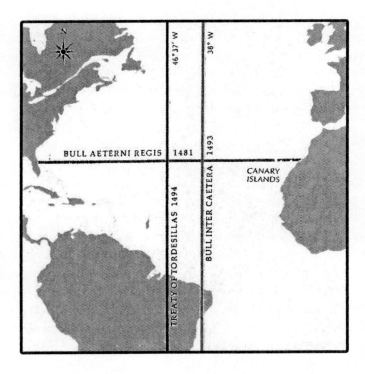

Demarcation lines according to papal bulls.
Paolo Emilio Taviani: "The Great Discovery" p. 57.

SYNOPSIS

In 1992 during the festivities for the celebration of the Quincentenary of the discovery of America, Prof. Marinella Bonvini Mazzanti, Associate Professor of History at the University of Urbino, Italy, discovered, researching through documents written after Columbus' return from the first voyage, that there was a fourth ship accompanying the expedition.

At the time Senator Emilio Paolo Taviani was recognized all over the world as the authority on Columbian studies and his books had been translated in all languages and shipped to schools and bookstores where the Quincentenary was celebrated.

Since the day Mrs. Stark received Prof. Mazzanti's book, she had the idea of researching more about this fourth ship directly in Santo Domingo. On January 17, 2004, while in Santo Domingo for three days visiting the Museum of the Royal Houses, the Maritime Museum, and the House of Diego Colón she found the picture of this fourth ship, which originally was a *"Fusta." Fusta* was a type of pirate ship used by the Portuguese during their raids along the African coast where there was no control and the Portuguese pirates could fill the cargo-hold with everything they could gather from their raids and sell for their own profits. It was a ship with very large cargo-hold that could also carry quite a bit of weight, up to forty men, and withstand strong winds.

By the time Columbus was ready to sail the Ocean Sea, many Africans and Mediterranean territories had become colonies under government regulations; so whoever wanted to continue piracy had to move their bases and Columbus' expedition would open new lands for such purpose as well as for legitimate business enterprises.

Apparently this "fourth ship" was not considered part of Columbus' official expedition, but simply an extra caravel financed and equipped by private entrepreneurs, who simply wanted to follow him of their own free will.

When, upon arrival to Hispaniola, Columbus' flagship *La Santa Maria"* was shipwrecked behind repair, Fort Navidad was built using all the wood that could be salvaged from it. So it is conceivable that Columbus would leave *La Fusta* for the 39 men he left there to continue the exploration of the island while he returned to Spain on *La Niña* and the brothers Pinzón on *La Pinta*.

SOURCES NOT MENTIONED IN FOOTNOTES

JOSE RAMON ESTELLA & JOSE ALLOZA VILLAGRASA
Historia gráfica de la República Dominicana

DOUGLAS T. PECK
Cristoforo Colombo, God's Navigator

ROBERT G. FERRIS
Explorers and Settlers

FCO. JOSE ARNAIZ, S.J.
Más Luces que Sombras

SAMUEL ELIOT MORISON
The European discovery of America

ROBERTO M. TISNÉS
Alejandro Geraldini

FRAY VICENTE RUBIO
Historia de los orígenes de la ciudad de Santo Domingo

BVG